"If Anne Rice and Chuck P
Christopher Zeischegg. *Com*
danger, horror, sex, the erotic
has taken queer literature and the vampire genre in a new and exciting direction."

– **JOE FILLIPONE,** author of *In the Tarot*

"A dark splatter punk novel for the LaCroix generation."

– **LUKA FISHER,** artist

"Seamlessly blends budding romanticism with a *Rules of Attraction*-like raucousness. Though decorated with things like sex, blood, and black metal, the meat of the book is tender."

– **CHAD FJERSTAD,** author of *Warship Satan*

"Christopher Zeischegg's first novel masterfully peels back a comfortable, familiar setting to reveal the blood and gore underneath. But the true horror is in their combination. Raw emotion and gut-wrenching violence are interspersed from page to page... The burgeoning trademark of his unique voice."

– **EVAN YEONG,** *CultureWarReporters.com*

"A brilliant debut that gnaws at the flesh... More than a love story, Zeischegg's novel is an undertow into the dark impulses of the human psyche, where he reveals an unsettling truth: that there is little that separates humanity from monsters."

– **ASHER YAP,** artist

"Young love, like poetry, is often the result of calamity... Christopher presents us with the protagonist of our past, a mirror for every young boy in service to their lust and in pursuit of its eternal exploitation."

– **DANIEL CROOK**

COME TO MY BROTHER

CHRISTOPHER ZEISCHEGG
AKA DANNY WYLDE

ISBN: 978-0-692-91949-1

Cover Design: Jared Rourke
Author Photo: Maggie West

Typeset in Garamond
Printed in the United States of America

File under:
Horror
Queer
Bildungsroman
Vampires

www.ChristopherZeischegg.com

A version of this manuscript was first published in 2013 by Queer Young Cowboys. The book you're holding now has been revised and updated by the author.

Also By Christopher Zeischegg

The Wolves that Live in Skin and Space
Body to Job

MIKA IS OLDER THAN I AM

THE SYMPHONY UPSTAIRS WAS COMPOSED OF voices and steps and bass from the speakers, blaring house music or some other form of EDM. In the bathroom below, it all sounded the same. Except the rhythm was thrown off by the gags of Peter's throat and the splash of his vomit hitting the sides of the toilet bowl.

***

I'd called Peter fifteen minutes before I'd planned to arrive, and I'd planned to arrive fashionably late. By the time I swung by his house, and saw that he was still undressed and barely conscious, I'd already received two voicemails from Mika. They reminded me of my promise to make an appearance at her twenty-sixth birthday party.

Because of this – because of my promise, because I'd spent the whole day in bed, shaking and gnawing on the inside of my cheeks, because I'd finally stopped crying and pulled myself together enough to be on the edge of socially acceptable, because I knew Mika would be the only face I'd recognize at the party, and that she'd be coked up or crashing, and most likely getting her pussy eaten, and really, because I was so fucking low on karma – I forced a pair of underwear on to Peter, and wrapped him in a robe.

We ended up at 314 Golden Avenue at 2:34 AM, and I found Mika draped around two blonde girls. She took turns exchanging saliva with the both of them. Once she noticed me, she smiled and motioned for me to bend down. She kissed me on the cheek.

"Happy birthday," I said.

"I thought you weren't going to make it," said Mika. "What happened to your neck?"

"Nothing." I stood and saw that Peter had fallen to the floor. The tip of his penis poked out the side of his underwear. One of the blonde girls pointed out that he was uncircumcised.

"Who's that?" Mika nodded towards Peter.

"A friend."'

Mika returned her attention to the blonde girls.

***

Ten minutes later, Peter leaned into me and did his best to yell over the music. "I think I'm going to throw up!" His eyes rolled back. He looked like he was trying to open his mouth.

I closed his jaw and dragged him through a door that was taped over with a sign that read, *OFF LIMITS*. The door lead down some stairs, to a bedroom with cream walls and to a whitewashed room with a small sink and toilet.

Peter's head landed between the toilet seat. He spewed forth.

ABBREVIATED HISTORY

PETER ATTENDED THE NEVADA COUNTY BRANCH of Sierra Community College during the Spring of 2002. So did I. He also signed up for English 1A and happened to sit directly across from me. That's when we first crossed paths.

I found common ground with Peter on the basis of our hate for Shakespeare.

"Nobody fucking talks like that."

Our get-to-know-each-other conversation happened outside, about a hundred yards from the classroom. Peter told me that his parents had recently died. He said that his father's lawyer had read him the will. "... My son will receive his inheritance ($1 million and my estate) upon the completion of four years of post-high school education..." Peter smoked a cigarette he'd hollowed out and filled with marijuana. I wasn't sure if that was why he was laughing. But he was.

"My dad didn't go to school," said Peter. "He was into real estate. Why the fuck, okay, like, why the fuck would I go to school?"

"You're in school," I said.

"That's what's so fucked up," he said.

Peter never showed signs of loss or depression at the death of his parents. At least, not that I could see. But he invited me to his house that night. We fell on to his leather couch. He pulled me on top of him. We made out for about half an hour. Then fifty other kids showed up at his door. They drank a lot of beer. Some fucked in his bathroom. I felt special because I became a part of it. The gatherings. The atmosphere of temporary belonging that I needed. Because I had lost someone too.

SOMETHING IN COMMON

I WAS SIX YEARS OLD AND HAD JUST MOVED TO A small town in the Sierra Nevada foothills. Daniel Brion was six years old and had lived on Mill Street his whole life when my family bought the house across from his.

Something familiar, almost immediate, caught my attention. It was the sounds. His house made the same sounds as mine, except backwards. I couldn't have heard them from inside my room. But I ventured out that first night, through the trimmed grass on our lawn and into the street. I was crying, because I always felt like crying on the nights before Daniel. On that particular night, I did as I felt.

I stared at the stars, because it was the first time in my life that I could see past the haze of urban pollution and into the heavens. I laid my back to the asphalt, and took in the sky and its million burning lights. My ears let in the sounds that carried over from my new home. They were the sounds of a grown man, yelling and screaming, and a grown woman, sobbing and begging. The sounds of my mother and father.

Then the sounds of someone else.

A house erupted from the other side of the street. I thought it was an echo – my parents' words taking up more space than what they deserved. But the words weren't the same and the voices changed, if only slightly. There was still a grown man. Still a grown woman. But the woman yelled and screamed, and the man sobbed and begged.

I sat up and shifted my stare to the new house. At the far end, where the lights were turned off, a window slid open and a boy peeked his head out. He turned back and forth, as if to look around, and tumbled on to the grass.

At that moment, I wanted to run. Though, when I planted my hands in the concrete, the boy had already stood up. I saw the stars glisten in the tears on his face. He walked towards me and kicked the ground with his feet. His head was pointed down, so that he could have only seen directly in front of him. Soon enough, I was only a few paces away and still sitting in the middle of the road.

He stopped in the center of Mill Street. I felt frozen. Unable to move, speak, or do anything but look him in the eyes. He stared back. We both stayed still long enough that the tears dried on his face.

"What are you doing?" he asked, and rubbed a hand under his nose.

It took a while for me to answer. But I told him the truth. "Looking up there." I pointed my index finger to the brightest ball of gas I could find.

"Oh," he said, and joined me. I knew that I didn't have to tell him why I sat in the middle of the road instead of lying tucked beneath the blankets of a warm bed. He knew because of the sounds. His house made them too.

On the ground, with his head next to mine, he told me his name was Daniel.

I traced an unknown constellation with my eyes and told him mine: David.

A GOOD HOST GIVES GOOD HEAD

PETER FINISHED VOMITING AND DROPPED TO the tile floor. I tried to flip him on his side, so that he wouldn't choke on any half-digested food that still waited to be shot out of his esophagus. But Peter brushed me away.

"I can do it," he said. "Just give me a minute."

I gave him a minute and then another. Peter managed to push himself up, so that his back was against the wall and his legs were sprawled out in front of him. He reached his hands into what would have been his pockets. It was the first time Peter realized that he wasn't wearing pants.

"Cool party," he said, and drooled all over his chest. The robe had more-or-less fallen off. "It's a costume thing, right?"

"No," I said, pissed.

"Where are my clothes?"

I leaned against the sink and crossed my arms. "I don't know."

Peter laughed in a drunk and near-passing out sort of way. "Wait, it's a costume party, right?"

My repeated, "No," was sharp and should have made the

point that I thought he wasn't being cute.

"Do you have a rash, like, on your neck? Or something?"

I didn't answer.

"Just give me my clothes." He was still laughing. Barely.

"Hey," said a voice from near the doorway.

I turned towards a boy, around eighteen years old. He had a faux hawk and a pierced lip, and was ridiculously attractive in a scene kind of way. I remembered seeing him when we first arrived at Mika's.

"You're not supposed to be down here. There was a sign." The boy pointed towards the door leading to the stairs.

"Sorry." I motioned towards Peter, who had begun to snore.

"I..." The boy sounded like he was trying to be stern. It wasn't working. Maybe he wasn't really upset. There was almost a kindness in his voice. Maybe it was something else. He kept looking at Peter and would only glance at me. He smiled every time we met eyes.

"Sorry," I said, again. "He had to..."

"It's okay," said the boy. "It's just that I'm Mika's roommate. It's her birthday."

I nodded.

"I'm looking out for everything. Making sure no one fucks up the place. So that Mika doesn't have to stress."

"I wasn't trying to fuck anything up," I said.

"Don't worry about it. This is my room, my bathroom." He extended his hand. "My name's Daniel."

My knees went weak. Suddenly, his hand seemed far away. My eyes blurred, and I didn't know if the room just looked like an earthquake from inside my head. Memories from the night before rushed at my head like a thunderstorm of unwanted thoughts.

I felt Daniel's hand on my own. But he wasn't the Daniel I wanted. He must have been trying to touch my face. Because my head was buried in my hands. My teeth came together, grinding. The boy in front of me, Daniel – but not my Daniel – kept saying, "It's okay." His voice was so assuring that I almost believed him.

He pulled my face towards him and pressed his lips to mine. His mouth tasted almost familiar. When he broke away to kiss my neck, I said, "I can't," and, "I'm sorry." But he kept holding me and telling me that everything would be okay.

He lead me into the next room. I fell on to his bed. My pants came off easily. He tugged at my penis – my limp penis. Tongued it. It should have felt good even if I didn't want it to. But I was so scared that I shrunk. My whole body shrunk. The same thing played over and over in my head. Forward and backward. The dirt fell and came back up. Under the dirt, I could see his face.

I miss him so much.

Where is he?

Gone.

But where is he?

I don't know.

You're the only one who knows.

In the ground?

Who put him there?

I'm sorry.

Who put him there?

I don't know.

It was you.

But I had to do it.

It was you.

I could see the ceiling when I opened my eyes. My cock felt warm and wet. A sensation crept through my body as I released into the mouth of a boy named Daniel. A boy I didn't even know.

He smiled at me and rubbed my stomach. I told him that I had to go.

"Why?"

"I have to mourn my friend."

The boy stopped smiling and no longer looked me in the eyes. His energy disappeared. A sadness came over him, like a veil of unwanted empathy.

I pulled up my pants and walked to the door. As I reached for the handle, he asked, "What happened?"

"I killed him."

WE NEVER CHOSE TO BE BROTHERS

THAT FIRST WEEK PASSED ON MILL STREET, AND with no more signs of Daniel. I spent two nights in the middle of the road, staring less at the stars and more at the house across the street. I waited for the window to open and for a boy to jump out. But the window stayed closed and I returned to bed each night, and plugged my ears with tissue paper so that I could go to sleep.

Then the second week came, and the first day of school. The town only had one Kindergarten class, and Daniel and I were both in it.

Daniel showed up to class with his left arm in a sling, and I knew why he hadn't come out the window the past two nights. He told me that he fractured his wrist while fighting off pirates. His description of one pirate was decidedly feminine, and matched that of a woman I met the following week when his family invited mine over for dinner. The woman he called Mommy.

***

"It seems like our kids have taken to each other," said Mr. Brion.

He ate from a plate of hot spaghetti that his wife had instructed him to make. "At school, and at church too."

"I know," said my mother, Cassandra Nevenhart. She always smiled in public, and considered the neighbor's house to be a public place. "Such a coincidence that we live across the street from each other."

Mrs. Brion apologized for the meal. "I thought my husband would follow the recipe for once." She laughed. "I should know better by now."

Mr. Brion sunk between his shoulders, and came back up only when my mother said, "Oh, I like the food."

"You don't have to pretend," said my father, Edward Nevenhart. "Just because they're neighbors." He smirked at Mrs. Brion, and went on to talk about all of the money he was supposedly making.

I was bored. So I twisted noodles around my fork, exchanged playful kicks with Daniel, and asked myself questions so that I could make up the answers. It was something I continued to do throughout my life. But the answers required less and less of my imagination.

Do you think Mrs. Brion is really a pirate?
Probably.
Why doesn't she wear an eye patch?
Not all pirates wear eye patches.
Where does she keep her ship?
In the creek behind her house?
Why would she hurt my friend?
I don't know.

I didn't have to ask anymore questions, because Daniel and

I were allowed to leave the table. We gave our hands more productive things to do, like line the living room floor with plastic army men.

***

The next year of our friendship turned to brotherhood when my father spent more time sleeping in Mrs. Brion's bed than his own. I hid behind my parents' door while he explained why.

"Because I'm bored. What do you want me to say, Cassandra? That it has nothing to do with you?"

The fight was gone from my mother's words by the time they reached her lips. "I just want what's best for our family."

"I want a divorce," said my father.

He swung the door open and into my face.

I woke up to my mother holding me under the fluorescent lights of the local Emergency Room. She smiled and wiped a blood stained tissue across my nose.

"Daniel's going to spend the night with us tonight," she said. "And Mr. Brion too."

They spent more than one night in our home. Mrs. Brion kicked her husband out and invited my father in instead. With nowhere else to go, Mr. Brion traveled the hundred yards it took to cross the street and end up on our front step. Daniel stood with him when he asked my mother if we could spare the couch for a night. My mother fell into his arms, and said, "Of course."

But no one took the couch. Daniel slept on a mattress next to mine. Mr. Brion took my mother's hand as she guided him towards her bed and laid him down beside her. They made sounds that night, my mother and Mr. Brion. But they were different from what I was used to.

There were no longer screams or verbal assaults. The cries and whimpers were gone too. All I could hear from my mother's room was the swell of heavy breath and the steady pulse of a rocking bed frame. Still, they were sounds I could fall asleep to.

The fact that my first restful night was spent with Daniel put something in my head that stayed there for a kind of eternity: he could take away those bits of sadness that hid in the walls and crept up on me whenever I felt the world had run out of people. Whenever I felt I was the only one left, unloved and uncared for.

With Daniel beside me, the warmth had returned. Or perhaps, it first appeared. It sat in my chest and poured energy through my limbs, and gave me some sense of life. It didn't matter if the rest of the world disappeared. There was at least someone left to share it with.

***

A note, signed by my father, appeared on our doorstep. It explained his decision to marry Mrs. Brion. In retaliation, my mother asked for Mr. Brion's hand in marriage. The act of jealousy seemed to work. My mother became Mrs. Brion, and Daniel's became Mrs. Nevenhart. Neither couple sold their house or moved away. We became neighbors, family, who never spoke to each other; never acknowledged each other's presence.

The new Mister and Misses Nevenhart didn't care about the custody of their children. So Daniel and I stayed in my mother's home. We didn't speak to our other parents. Occasionally, we would see them in the driveway, walking to or from their car. Per my mother's advice, we pretended that no one was there.

None of it seemed to matter. Daniel and I created our own world. A fort of sheets and household structures grew in our room. We rarely left, but to eat, use the bathroom, and go to school. In that special place, we could turn ourselves and our surroundings into anything we wanted. We could scale the walls of a forbidden castle or sail the seas of uncharted waters. We could fight off the hordes of barbarian armies or secure a tropical paradise all to ourselves.

We shared a year of our lives in that place. And we discovered a bond that would carry us past it.

FOOD

A SHARP COLD RAN THROUGH MY LEG AS I TOOK the first step. I was alone in the staircase between the upper and lower floors of Mika's apartment. A faint light trickled from a crack in the door above. It allowed me to make out the shape of my feet. They looked thin, bony, and naked. But I remembered arriving in socks and shoes.

It wasn't so long ago that I'd left the boy behind in his room. He'd taken off my pants. When they'd stuck near my ankles, he must have removed my shoes too.

The denim against my thighs assured me that I hadn't wandered away in only a shirt. But my shoes were still scattered across the floor, near the boy's bed. I turned myself around and took the single step back to the floor.

The bedroom door opened with the turn of a handle. I saw the boy, Daniel, knelt at the base of his bed. He looked up as I neared him. Then, as if startled to see me, he slid backwards in one, quick motion. His hands trembled. His voice seemed struck with fear when he asked, "What are you going to do?"

"I just came back for my shoes," I said.

He crawled backwards again, and continued to shake. It occurred to me that it might have had something to do with what I'd mentioned before leaving the first time. My confession, of sorts. The fact that I'd told him I killed my best friend.

I'd said it so carelessly and without the emotional context. But hadn't I been falling apart right before? When he'd laid me on his bed and taken me in his mouth? Hadn't I given him the chance to ask what was wrong before he chose fellatio as the cure?

I bent down to retrieve my shoes, and looked at the boy with a simple curiosity. Then a tense alertness came over me. I imagined myself in attack position, ready to pounce on my prey. A hunger gripped me like I'd never felt before. My eyes became slaves to some dormant instinct. They searched the boy, and paid special attention to the pulse beneath his skin. They traced the arteries in his arms and followed them to the pump and swell at his neck. They made their mark before I'd even left my feet. Before I'd pushed off and come crashing down.

He thrashed his arms and jerked away from my touch. His head pushed through the plaster as I trapped him against the wall. My teeth fell over his flesh, and I dug in. He tore open and sprayed my mouth with blood. I kept at it, even when my throat had overflowed. His blood poured over the sides of my lips, stained my shirt, and kept dripping. I felt his insides warm my groin and stream further down my legs, until they puddled at my feet.

After a time, the blood ceased to flow. My lips peeled back, and I filled my lungs with cold air. The act was done, and I felt a cloud lift from my head.

A moment came, in which I was able to dwell on what I'd done. I asked myself the burning question that erupted to the surface and drowned out all other thought.

What the fuck just happened?

I didn't say it out loud, because there was no one to answer. Peter had passed out behind the bathroom door. Even if he stood beside me, what explanation could he have given? Not the one I began to construct. No, not construct. It was formed long ago.

I held my eyes shut, and prayed for the nightmare to be over. But it stayed.

My fingers traced the ridge of my teeth and found my canines, doubled in length, whittled down to sharp points at the end – razor tips that punctured my skin with the slightest bit of pressure.

I denied my sense of touch and hoped that sight would prove my reality as something different. I dragged myself towards the bathroom door and heaved it open; threw my hands up to the sink and pulled my body towards the mirror.

My eyes shot open, and I stared into the dimly lit reflection. The face that stared back looked almost like my own, but drowned in a red-splattered mask and with a pair of fangs beneath my lips.

In an instant, I knew what I'd become. I knew it all the more, because I'd seen it in my friend the night before.

I looked to the wound he'd left on my neck, and wiped away the blood that sprayed it over; peered again at the mirror, to where the marks should have been. All I found was smooth, flawless skin.

REUNION

I'D SEEN MIKA A COUPLE OF NIGHTS BEFORE HER birthday party. Her catering service had been hired by the company I worked for.

She was all smiles when I walked towards her, to the table she'd prepared with *hors d'oeuvres*.

"She was cute," said Mika.

"Who?" I asked, because I hadn't eaten all day, and my head wasn't clear enough to assume the obvious.

"The girl pounding your ass about twenty minutes ago. Who else would I be talking about?"

"You're sneaking out on the job?" I said through a mouthful of food.

"Not sneaking," said Mika. "Madame Rose let me watch."

Madame Rose was the pseudonym for a tall, blonde woman who spent her days thinking of ways to tie people up. She was a director at Fetisynth, one of the world's leading manufacturers of adult entertainment. They produced hardcore BDSM porn – ropes, whips, gags, and penetration.

I often performed for Fetisynth. It was my only source of income. The production, on to which Mika had stumbled, featured a petite, young woman who fucked me up the ass with a strap-on dildo.

But none of that – Mika, my work, or getting fucked in the ass – had anything to do with how my night had gone so wrong. I was just in the city when I'd left Fetisynth. And the city was where the rest had taken place.

***

I'd parked my car in a garage, several blocks from work. On the way to pick it up, I passed a man with an outstretched cup. He smelled like cat piss and sat beside a cardboard sign that read, *Hungry*, in scribbled ink.

What should I eat for dinner?
I don't know. Why didn't you take a plate from Mika?
Fuck. Why didn't I?
There's always that Thai place on the way home.
Yeah, but it'll probably be closed by the time I get there.
Maybe you should ask the bum what he would eat.
Maybe if I was an asshole.

I didn't have time to be an asshole, or at least play out the part. When I looked to the cat-piss-smelling man, he was being hoisted to his feet by someone younger. The young man removed his coat and wrapped it around the shivering vagrant.

The act of kindness shouldn't have been so unusual. But I watched, as if it were a spectacle. I was entranced by the young man's movements. The way he slid the coat off his back and removed the sleeves from his arm, the gait of his step as he walked along and motioned for the bum to follow. It was as if I could predict the way his body would shift in its motion. As if I'd seen it all before in a dream.

But I couldn't see the young man's features. Not in the dark or from where I stood. I only meant to follow him into the light, so that I could catch a better look. But the street lamps were broken. For a block or two, or more.

I couldn't figure out my motivation, but I walked the same path and turned down the same streets as the homeless man and good samaritan. When they started up the steps of an old apartment complex, I felt foolish for having followed them so far. I was sure they'd disappear into the building, and that I'd be left without a face to match the young man's body. I was sure he'd end up another unanswered question that would come back one night to keep me from falling asleep.

I looked around for a street sign or landmark – something to tell me where I was. I wandered back and forth, and tried to decipher the best route back to my car. There was no one in sight. No shadow appeared to move. I was in the middle of a city teeming with overpopulation, but saw no sign of life.

I sat on the steps of the apartment complex and pulled out my phone. There was a sound from behind me, like the creak of an open door. Before I could turn around, I felt a foot hit the center of my back. My body toppled forward and I landed on the sidewalk.

The silhouette of a man towered above me. For a moment, I took it to be a ghost. But the ghost spoke and grabbed hold of my jacket, and pulled me towards its face. I could see its eyes, skin, and mouth, and that they were all very much human.

"Why are you following me?" asked the man.

I made a noise, like a frightened animal, and believed that I'd be beaten.

But the man loosened his grip on my jacket, and said, in a voice that nearly calmed me, "David?" He said my name again, but no longer as a question. "David."

I needed a moment to put his face together. When I'd taken it in, and looked back at his blue eyes, I saw my old friend, Daniel Brion.

There was a burning from inside my chest – a response to a loss that I'd taken for granted; one that seemed like it might have been found. I wanted to reach out and let Daniel know the moment meant more to me than silence. But I was burdened by a hurt from our past.

Daniel wrapped his arms around me and held me close. "Where have you been?" I asked, whispered in his ear.

He pulled away. I could see a tension in his jaw. It looked like he wanted to speak but couldn't.

"Fuck, it doesn't matter," I said. "You're alive, and –"

"I guess so," said Daniel.

He waited a moment, and then asked me to come inside.

***

"Whoa," I said. "You live here?" It was impossible to tell from building's exterior, but Daniel's apartment was spotless and appeared to be a product of the world's upper echelon of interior designers.

"Yes," said Daniel.

"So are you, like, rich now?"

He shrugged, and set his keys down in a ceramic bowl – an art piece, maybe. Something designed to appear as if it was once alive. "Tell me how you've been," he said, as if we'd just spent some time apart and only needed to catch up. "You live in the city?"

"Yeah," I said, and then corrected myself. "I mean, not live. Work. I go to school at UC Santa Cruz, so I live in the dorms."

I followed Daniel towards his living room and stepped on to the marble floor. There was a sound of running water from nearby.

"You were following me for a while," said Daniel. "Why didn't you say something?"

"I didn't know it was you," I said, and was about to explain further. But there was a photo, on a table near the couch, that caught my attention. It showed Daniel with his arm around a woman. I didn't recognize her. "Who is..."

Daniel cut me off. "My other guest?"

I nodded, even though I'd meant to ask about the woman in the photo.

"I don't know his name," said Daniel. "He just looked like he could use a second chance. At the very least, I could make him a meal."

I nearly laughed at Daniel's new-found sense of charity. I hadn't known him to be the type of person to help a stranger. But the sincerity in his voice kept me biting my tongue. "When did you become the philanthropist?"

Daniel smiled, and it seemed like the first time since he'd found me on the steps. "It's probably not what you think."

"Well, it's very Mother Theresa of you," I said.

"David," he said, and looked me directly in the eye. "I want to show you something. It's very possible that you're not going to like it."

"Then why would you show it to me?"

"If you disapprove, it will only be at first," he said. "Of that, I'm sure." He motioned for me to come with him as he walked towards a door on the far wall. The sound of running water grew louder. It seemed like we were headed towards the bathroom.

Daniel turned to me. "All I ask is that you watch and don't be frightened. What you see might help to clear things up."

"Can't we just talk?" I said. He acted like there was nothing wrong between us. It was hard for me to keep playing along. "I mean, I can't believe I'm here. With you. Everyone back home thinks your dead. I thought you were dead."

Daniel put a finger to his lips, as if he'd told me to be quiet.

I didn't know what he'd meant to show me, but I tried to make a guess. "Look, I'm not here to put guilt on you, or anything," I said. "Things are obviously different now. Maybe you're into older guys, because there's one in the shower. That's cool if you are. But I don't need to see you with him, or whatever."

Daniel gave me a look, like I'd offended him. Then he opened the door to his steam filled bathroom. The shower was on, and I could hear the homeless man inside, humming a tune I didn't recognize. The song, coupled with the splash of water, seemed to mask the sound of Daniel's feet.

The shower door swung open. Soon after, I saw a splash of blood paint the walls. I jumped back and lost my footing on the wet tile, and fell into a corner near the toilet.

"Fuck," I said out loud, and couldn't manage anything else.

Daniel wrenched his head back from a geyser on the old man's neck. He looked at me, and his eyes became something to focus on – a point or two of clarity amidst the chaos of his violence. I slipped into the blue, and felt my brain become a kind of numb.

Then a thud hit my ears, and I saw the homeless man's body drop from Daniel's arms. The shower poured streaks through the blood on my old friend's face, as if to exfoliate his savage exterior.

"David," he said, and pronounced my name with such tenderness. "Everything I wanted when we were young is real. I didn't plan for you to be here tonight. But it's no accident."

"It's not?" I said, and felt a fear across my skin.

"No," said Daniel. "You were meant to see this. Because you

were meant to share my gift. I know it's hard to accept at first. But I'm giving you a choice, however forced it may seem."

I knew that Daniel had overindulged his fantasies when we were teenagers. But he'd since gone off the deep end. I'd just watched him kill a man with his bare teeth.

Daniel moved towards me and continued. "The choice is to change and live out your greatest dreams, or..." He motioned to the corpse that he'd left on the floor.

I reached for the towel hanger above me, and tried to pull myself on to my feet. But my weight was too much. The towel hanger ripped from its place on the wall. I fell back to the floor.

Daniel knelt in front of me and took my head in his hands. "This part's not so bad," he said. "I promise."

I kicked at him and screamed for help, but Daniel didn't loosen his hold. He tried to kiss me, and bit gently at my lip. Then he moved his mouth to right below my ear. His tongue found my neck, and I no longer knew whether to struggle. I continued, though maybe not as hard.

Then I felt a sudden pain, and knew that he'd bitten into me. I tried to wrench my neck to the side, as if I could crush his head between my shoulder and temple. But his jaw was stuck in place. Some part of me drained through the punctures in my skin. Daniel slurped it up with his tongue.

I swept my hands along the floor, and found a long, metal cylinder with a jagged tear at one end. It was the fallen towel hanger.

I swung the makeshift weapon against Daniel's ribs, but he remained clamped on to my flesh. Another strike found the back of his skull. It carried enough force to loosen his bite. I was given a few moments to scramble towards the living room without Daniel as a parasite.

He was back on his feet by the time I reached the door. I swung the towel hanger again, but with both hands, and cracked him across the face. His head hit the wall, and he collapsed.

My adrenaline pumped, and I teetered between defense mechanisms of fight and flight. I allowed fight one more chance to prove itself, and stabbed at Daniel, as if the towel hanger were a knife. The metal fell towards the center of Daniel's chest, but strayed slightly to one side. Bubbles appeared in a froth of blood that spilled up from his wound.

I dropped to my knees and then further. My arm draped across his chest. Daniel's face rolled over, and his eyes met mine. We laid in accidental embrace for the last moments of his life.

***

I spent hours mixing my tears with the dark pools that had accumulated on the bathroom tile. Guilt poured through my veins and out of every pore. I left the apartment, and wandered outside. The fog seemed to be missing, but no stars took its place. The sky looked black and endless.

There was a plot of dirt behind the building, like a garden that had never been given the chance to grow. I saw a rusted shovel, half-buried in the earth. It seemed like a tool that had been put there just for me.

I dug a space for Daniel's body, and discovered more of what he'd done. There were bones and rotting flesh just beneath the softened dirt.

Still, I carried on, and hoped to put my old friend to rest. I wrapped his body in sheets and towels, and buried him in the ground, beside the cat-piss-smelling man.

IF PETER LEARNED TO TRUST HIMSELF

PETER WOKE UP. "BRO," HE SAID. "I THINK I'M really fucked up." His head hung low, and he rubbed his eyes. "Someone must have slipped something in my drink."

I scrubbed my face and arms with soap and warm water from the sink. The blood was almost gone from my skin.

"I have to get out of here," said Peter.

"Yeah."

I noticed the mess I'd made in the bathroom, and wasn't sure if Peter did too.

"Just don't eat me," said Peter, in a slur. I couldn't tell if he was joking. He stood and walked to the door with relative ease. I watched him step off the tile and on to the blood-soaked carpet of the adjacent room. "Christ," he said. "It's too early for this Halloween shit."

I began to come to terms with the inevitable. Peter would realize that there was a dead body several feet from where he stood. He'd scream, run, and tell everyone that I killed Mika's roommate. I'd have no explanation when the police came to find me drenched in evidence of first-degree murder.

I thought of running. But I was tired, and almost believed it would be better to sleep away the next several decades behind bars.

Peter asked me a simple favor. "Drive me home. Please. I'm way to high to be here, and I don't even know where *here* is."

"Yeah, okay," I said, and waited for him to change his mind. But Peter didn't freak out, or do much of anything. He could barely open his eyes.

I lead him up the stairs to Mika's living room. We didn't stop to acknowledge anyone. Not the dwindling crowd of hipsters, or the couple groping on the couch, or even the birthday girl, who appeared to be receiving cunnilingus in her sleep. We left the party through the front door. No one tried to stop us.

I dropped Peter off in front of his apartment, drove away into the night, and found my way to bed before the sun came up.

BELATED BIRTHDAY PRESENT

ONE WEEK AFTER MY SEVENTH BIRTHDAY, I LEFT for school on my own. Daniel stayed behind with a common cold – something I'd kept clear of, despite spending the typical twenty-three-and-a-half hours a day by his side.

It wasn't so bad. I just ate lunch alone and spent recess in my head.

On the ride home, I drew pictures on the fogged up windows. I allowed my imagination to turn my thoughts away from the empty seat beside me. But the rain outside reminded me that I wasn't exiting a submarine destined for Atlantis. Just a rusted, yellow school bus stopped half a block from my house.

As I splashed through the puddles on the way to my front door, I saw a pair of soaked Italian loafers step into view. They accompanied a faintly familiar voice. "Hey buddy."

I looked up and through a sheet of thick rain. A man stood with a disintegrating newspaper over his head. He held a plastic-wrapped box with a pink ribbon stapled to the top.

"It's me," he said. "You remember your old man?" His face brought back several memories. They were of the neighbor across the street. The one my mother told me not to speak to. "I got you a birthday present," he said, and sounded disappointed. "At least I remembered your birthday, right?" He knelt and offered me the box. "Come on. Let's get out of this mess."

I took the box from him and sprinted towards the house. The front door was made of wood, and had swollen with the rain. But I managed to get it open with the help of my father's giant hands. We both stumbled inside, and tracked water into the foyer.

"Edward, you prick!" My mother's voice erupted from the living room. "Get out of my house!"

It was strange to see my father cower, and to hear my mother come off so loud.

"I'm just here to give David a present," said my father. "I swear. I didn't even know you were home."

"Oh, so now you have a son?" said my mother. "How convenient for you. The same week I decide to ask for child support."

"It's not like that," said my father.

My parents continued to argue while I tore open the box. There was plastic, cardboard, bubble wrap, and finally a package labeled Pink Passion Dual Pleasure Anal Balls. I held the thing for several moments, and examined all its sides and oddly pictured instructions.

A silence reached my ears. My mother stared at me with a horrified expression.

"Are you retarded?" screamed my mother.

My father took a look at what I was holding. "Oh God." He stepped backwards and put his hands up, as if to brace himself for an attack. "That... Those... They're for Lindsay."

My father had been in the giving spirit. He'd mail-ordered two separate packages. The first, a set of G.I. Joe army men, was meant to be my birthday present. He'd ordered the second as a surprise for his wife, and to help with their sex life. It seemed that he'd mixed up the packages. And so I was given the most perplexing gift of my seventh birthday.

Despite my father's apologies, he was thrown out of the house. My mother stood by the door and peered out our small window. By the time she turned around, her breath had returned to the rate I was accustomed to. Her voice, too, held the soft cadence that I'd come to know so well.

"I'm sorry," she said. "You won't have to worry about him again."

But my mother was wrong. My father returned the following day with the intent to inflict his presence on my childhood. He came with a lawyer, police officer, and all the makings of a custody battle to come. His wife, Lindsay, stayed behind. But my father claimed that she wanted her son back too.

Our parents ended up in court. A judge ordered Daniel and I to attend weekly counseling sessions with a family therapist. But he didn't tell us that our therapist had been fighting a losing battle with brain cancer. Whatever relationship we were able to establish with Dr. Featherly was destroyed when she died a month-and-a-half into our sessions.

Before she passed, Dr. Featherly suggested a trial-run of a custody situation, in which Daniel and I would spend every Wednesday night and every other weekend with my father and his mother. It was the only suggestion, and so the judge ordered it into effect.

Every Wednesday and every other weekend, Daniel and I would pack our bags, as if we were about to go out of town. But we'd just cross the street. As pointless as it seemed, it was something our parents could agree on. We made camp at one house and then, several days later, tore down to move next door.

It worked for a few years. Then Daniel and I reached the age at which our individual privacy started to become a concern.

***

I was twelve years old, and at my mother's house, working on some homework. I asked Mr. Brion for help, because I knew that he was good at math. We puzzled over basic algebra on the kitchen table.

Daniel stayed in our room. He was allowed enough time, on his own, to break away from his studies and practice more recreational pursuits.

When I finished my homework, I found Daniel where I'd last seen him. Though, his pants were down and his penis was fully erect. A string of pink balls hung from his asshole. I recognized something in his hand that I'd stashed away years before: a worn package still clearly labeled Pink Passion Dual Pleasure Anal Balls.

My parents had been so overwhelmed that they'd never thought to take the box away from me. I hid my accidental birthday present in my bedroom closet. It only took five years for Daniel to dig it up, and less than thirty minutes for him to realize its intended use.

We never mentioned the incident to our parents. But it was clear that we needed our own space.

In order for Daniel and I to have our own rooms, one of us had to move across the street. Daniel volunteered. I defaulted to stay where I was. We were still able to see each other whenever we wanted. Our relationship only changed to be less like brothers and more like close friends.

MESSAGES

IT WAS NEAR PITCH BLACK WHEN I OPENED MY eyes. The only light flashed sporadically from somewhere on the floor.

My right arm fell from the mattress. I pressed my palm against the carpet. Amidst the textbooks and crumpled articles of clothing, I found a thin piece of plastic, my phone. It vibrated. Someone was calling. By the time I brought the device to my ear, the call had ended.

A small message popped up on the screen. It said that I had three missed calls, two voicemails, and even more unanswered texts.

I dropped the phone back on the floor.

What day is it?

Friday. I think.

That can't be right.

We are the same person, both confused.

If it's Friday, we've missed class and bailed on a shoot.

But if tomorrow's Saturday, there's less immediate responsibility.

What day is it really?

Monday.

That's what I thought.

I'd slept through three classes. The realization would have usually accompanied a mild state of panic, but I knew that school was the least of my worries.

I flipped a switch, and a small desk lamp flared up on the night stand beside me. The glow was just enough to light every wall of my dorm room. Everything was the way I'd left it: a splintered, wooden dresser at the foot of my bed and a small Ikea desk propped up in the corner. The rest was on the floor.

I sat at my desk and in front of my laptop. My internet browser was open to MySpace. I clicked refresh and saw that I had a few new messages. One was from a stranger, a girl with just one picture and some links to a hooker website. The next was from Louis, an androgynous-looking boy from my Queer Film class.

My video diary for Film 170c is due tomorrow. You have to be in it. No one else will get naked for me. Please?

You can just stop by my dorm tonight. I'm throwing a get-together thing. There's free beer.

Come over whenever. I need to film you doing something unusual. Without clothes on. I want to show my professor the kind of people I hang out with.

What's your # again?

I deleted Louis' message, and figured that he'd be banging on my door within the hour. If he convinced me to leave my room, he'd probably be disappointed with my nude exposition on how to drink his alcohol.

There was one more message. From Peter.

Where were we last night? I'm watching the news, and some fucked up murder happened on Golden Avenue, in SF. They're flashing this kid's face all over. He looks really fucking familiar. Can't really remember what happened.

I left you a voicemail. Sorry I sound like shit. But call me.

My chest tightened. I grabbed my cell phone and reminded myself, repeatedly, that twenty-year-olds rarely succumbed to heart attacks.

The screen lit up with the same message as before: three missed calls and two voicemails.

I listened to my voicemail.

"Uh, David. This is still your number, right? Let's pretend it is. Let's pretend we're having a conversation and you ask me, 'Peter, how are you?' I'd say, 'Not good. Like, really fucking, um, bad.' Bro, just call me. I'm going to hang up now."

Peter did sound like shit – like he was hungover or still drunk. Maybe on downers. But I could hear a fear in his voice. It was contagious. My heart beat faster by the time I listened to the next voicemail.

"David, it's Mika." She sounded like she was crying. "I need to talk to you." There was a long pause. "Just call me, okay?"

My phone vibrated before the message was through. It was Mika. Calling in real time.

I answered. "Hello?"

"David..."

"I was about to call you," I said, and tried to pretend that I didn't know why she was upset. "Are you okay?"

"I don't think so," she said. "Has anyone talked to you?"

"Anyone, like who?"

"I wanted to get a hold of you first. So you wouldn't freak

out. I know that you didn't do anything, but maybe you saw someone. Something."

"Mika, what's wrong?" I said, and felt like a piece of shit.

"Something happened to Daniel. The guy I live with. Lived with. Fuck..."

"I might have met him."

"He's dead," said Mika.

"Dead?"

"Someone killed him. In my apartment."

"Killed him?"

"I told the cops the name of everyone I remember being there last night. But it was my birthday, and I wasn't exactly lucid, or whatever."

I tried to be supportive. "It's going to be okay, Mika. None of this is your fault."

"Can you just tell the police if you saw something? Even if it doesn't seem like a big deal, just tell them."

"Yeah, okay."

"Didn't you bring a friend?" she asked.

"I was with him most of the night," I said, and felt somehow good for telling the truth.

"Can I have his name? He might have seen something."

"Uh, yeah, it's Peter."

"Peter," said Mika. "What's his number?"

There was a knock at my door.

"His number," I said. "I'll text it to you."

I heard, from outside my room, "I know you're in there, David. I can hear you talking to someone. And your MySpace says you're online." The voice sounded like Louis'.

I didn't catch every word from Mika, but she said, "... at Angela's, so text it to her too."

"Mika, I know this is bad timing, but I have to call you back," I said. "Someone's here."

"The police?"

"Yeah," I said, and knew that it was just my classmate outside the door. "I think so. I'll tell them everything I can remember. Take care of yourself, okay? It'll be alright."

"This is so fucked up," said Mika.

"I'll call you tomorrow, okay?"

She hung up.

To quell the knocking at my door, I swung it open, and said, "I was on the phone."

Louis stood with a camcorder in hand, ready to record my emergence from the small box I called home. "You have to come over," he said. "It's been really boring so far."

"Why would I come over if it's boring?"

Louis turned off the camera. "Please. I have to turn in this project tomorrow. I'll trade with you. Crew on whatever short film you have coming up."

"Fine," I said, because of course I was going with him. It was better than getting arrested whenever the cops decided to show up.

Louis smiled and shoved the camera back in my face. "Okay, I want to introduce you first. So talk to me while we're walking."

I followed Louis as he strolled backwards through the maze of the UC Santa Cruz, Porter Residence Hall. "What do you want me to say?"

"Tell me your name and stuff."

"I'm David." Pause. "Nevenhart."

"And what do you do?" said Louis.

"I'm a film student."

"And..."

"What?"

"Come on," he said. "Tell everyone how you're a porn star."

"I'm not a porn star."

"But you do porn, right? You fuck on camera?" Louis broke from his interview. "Wait, before you say anything, can you just make sure to repeat the question in all your answers? In case I need to edit out my voice."

I diverted my attention to the stairwell door. It burst open and two police officers walked through. Louis stopped recording and searched his pockets for gum to cover the booze on his breath. I stared straight ahead. My legs began to weaken. A tear formed in the corner of my eye and rolled down my cheek as the men in uniform passed by.

It was a strange feeling that came next. My thoughts disintegrated at a frenetic pace, and I watched the flesh beneath the cops' collars.

My mouth churned with saliva.

NOT QUITE A STAR

I SAT ON MY MOTHER'S COUCH AND STARED AT A piece of paper signed by the Dean of Admissions at UC Santa Cruz. It was my acceptance letter. The first ticket I had out of the small town I grew up in.

I'd wanted to leave so badly. I couldn't even think of waiting out the summer.

The next morning, I asked my mother for enough money to pay the first month's rent on an apartment in Santa Cruz. She said, "No," and her explanation seemed practical enough. She'd set aside a certain amount of money for my education, and didn't want to see it squandered before I'd made it to my first class.

But I wasn't about to give up.

Later in the day, I sat with my father, who still lived across the street. I'd decided on a point of leverage. My father hadn't exactly been the ideal parent. Any points he did score, Daniel was the one to witness them. Not me. I tried to push the point home a number of times.

My father didn't seem to catch on. But he still looked uncomfortable. I was pretty sure I did too. We hadn't had many real conversations over the years. It was almost like he wanted to pay me to shut up.

He wrote me a check for fifteen hundred dollars, and then escaped to his room for the night. It was the last time I saw him before I left. He already knew about my plans, so it didn't seem necessary to say goodbye.

I deposited the check, packed a suitcase, gave my mother a hug, and drove three-and-a-half hours to my destination: a studio apartment just north of downtown Santa Cruz. It was the cheapest place I could find while scouring the internet for a few hours prior to leaving. The taste of independence was enough for me to welcome it as home.

I didn't do much the first week in my apartment. I'd raced away from my mother's nest to hole up in a room and watch movies. Occasionally, I'd wander outside to look for food.

The pros of my new lifestyle were thwarted when I checked my bank account. I calculated how much I could spend before the next month's rent was due. It was less than zero dollars. I needed a job and a paycheck before the next three weeks were through.

I'd had one job prior, as a clerical assistant for a doctor friend of my mother's. It was the only mark on my resume other than some community college courses. So I felt less-than-confident flaunting my work experience in an interview.

I opted for what I thought would be the easiest means of income, and applied to several coffee shops in the downtown area. Few were hiring. The ones that were said to come back later, but wouldn't tell me when.

I sat in my apartment and scanned online job listings for any way to prevent myself from crawling back to my mother's, broke and defeated.

The first glimpse of hope came packaged in an ad listed under *Miscellaneous Jobs/Gigs*. A photographer named Thomas had posted a request for men to pose nude for his upcoming art show. He wanted the guys to be young and covered in ink or piercings. He offered forty dollars as payment.

The money wasn't much. But all I had to do was get naked. I was at a point in my life where I was down for almost anything, especially if it seemed unconventional or wrong in the eyes of people like my parents. The problem was my lack of tattoos and the fact that I only had two piercings: horizontal barbells shoved through my nipples. All the guys on Thomas' website had way more metal in their skin.

Why did I even bother? Because it gave me an idea: fake it.

I owned a few black pens and had plenty of time on my hands. The second-hand experience I'd gathered watching kids ink themselves up in high school led me to believe that I could pull off a passable replica of real-life, fuck-up body art. Because I wasn't an artist. At least, not the kind who knew how to draw. The best I could hope for was that my fake tattoo would look intentionally wrong. I stayed up all night and tried to think of an idea, but couldn't come up with one original piece. So I succumbed to blatant thievery. I copied the worst tattoo I could think of, and stole the story behind it too.

The photo I emailed to Thomas showed me in the nude and with a diagonal line streaked across my torso. In the accompanying text, I explained how I obtained the piece of work. It was a true story, just not mine. I'd witnessed the event about a year prior while hanging out with one of Peter's friends. Though, to Thomas, I was the one who'd formed a Dextromethorphan-inspired pact with a best friend. The agreement allowed my friend to design my first tattoo with a felt tip marker. Whatever my friend decided to draw, I would have it etched over by a real tattoo artist. The result was a permanent line strewn across my chest and stomach.

I told Thomas that it was a conceptual piece – a work that based its aesthetic on personal significance. He must have bought the lie, because I received a response within the hour. Thomas wanted to set up a shoot. We exchanged phone numbers and talked on the phone long enough for me to feel confident that he wasn't trying to kidnap or rape me. I took down the address for an abandoned warehouse in San Francisco, and met up with him at our appointed time.

The problem was the summer rain. I walked from my car to the front of the warehouse, and my shirt became drenched. I felt foolish. It was only a matter of time before I would remove my clothes in front of Thomas, and reveal a splotch of black ink smeared across my chest.

The photographer readied his lens. I was already nervous, because I'd never been naked on camera before, let alone tried to model. But there was an extra bit of stress, because of what I'd done. I began to strip out of my shirt, and stood frozen with the fabric pulled over my head. It was like I was trying to hide from the minor shame I'd brought on to myself.

Thomas laughed. Not too hard, but enough for my to understand his amusement. "You can take it off," he said.

I did as he suggested. Thomas lowered his camera, and asked, "What's going on here? Did Mitch put you up to this?"

"I don't know anyone named Mitch," I said, and shook my head. There was a bout of awkward silence. Then I delivered my explanation.

Thomas was still smiling when I finished my apologies. He didn't send me packing. Instead, he walked me through the rest of the shoot. He was intrigued, or something, and seemed to misinterpret my poor financial situation as a burning desire to break into the art modeling world. I left the shoot with a sheet full of contacts – artist friends of Thomas'; people he claimed would be in need of someone like me.

I took full advantage. After a day of phone calls, I'd lined myself up some gigs stripping off my clothes for artists of every medium. Before the month was through, I had enough money to stay in my apartment. There was even some left over for me to eat, though barely. It was all I needed to get by before school started up again.

I'd just begun to work, and wasn't on the lookout for a change of career. But I received an unusual request one day, and it was followed by another.

A man called me, per the recommendation of a mixed-media specialist in Oakland. He said that he belonged to a group of men that met about every other week to hold life drawing sessions. They always hired a model. But their theme was more particular than most. Each of the models would be tied in a Japanese style of rope bondage – what he referred to as *shibari*. The man assured me that all measures would be taken to ensure my safety.

The more he explained, the more I became comfortable with the idea. I'd grown used to exhibiting my body in such a short period of time. But up until that point, the work had never taken on a sexual context. Rope bondage, the man explained, was inherently erotic. Those who attended the life drawing courses sought to create erotic imagery. The fact that I was asked to be their muse gave me a strange sort of confidence – something I hadn't felt in a while.

The following week, I met with eleven men in an art studio overlooking San Francisco's Mission Street. One man called himself a rigger, and he seemed responsible for tying me up.

The other ten were art hobbyists – middle-aged homosexuals with disposable incomes. They made no attempts to hide their voyeurism. Sure, the art was part of the process. But each man seemed to fulfill another desire by watching my bound flesh. It was overwhelming at first, but I became at ease with their honesty. I wasn't a piece of meat to be torn apart by their eyes. Instead, I was made to feel revered for simply existing.

Still, I'd never been tied up. So I was beyond nervous when it came time to assume my first pose. The rigger had me put my arms behind my back. He tied rope around my hands and arms, and over my shoulders. He explained what he was doing each step of the way, as if it would ease my worries to understand the process. At some point, I closed my eyes and blocked out the sound of his voice. I focused on the placement of rope across my skin. It was like my discomfort evolved into pure sensation. I fell into something like a meditative state.

While splayed nude across the floor in a twist of taut, hemp twine, my mind settled in a place just right for the cultivation of a certain kind of pleasure. In short, my cock was hard within five minutes of my final position.

I would have gotten over my embarrassment and perhaps come to some realization about the way my body worked. But it just so happened that my erection became the catalyst for a new opportunity.

One of the artists approached me after the session. He'd noticed my rapid increase in blood flow, and told me that I would be great for a project his friend was working on. It was a new website for a company called Fetisynth.

Before I could get in a word, he asked me about my sexual orientation.

"What does that have to do with anything?" I asked.

"Well, it's a porn site. You'd have to fuck girls. At least, let them fuck you."

His response had me dumbfounded. I understood that my participation in the art session was somewhat sexual. But, in my mind, it was still a far way off from porn. I wasn't fondled, and there certainly wasn't any sex. More than that, I'd never been with a girl. Sure, I'd fooled around with some girlfriends in high school, but never to the point of intercourse. It wasn't that I didn't find them attractive. The opportunity had never presented itself.

Trying something new, for money, mostly sounded like a good idea. But everyone had limits. I just wasn't sure if mine had been reached.

The man slipped me a card with his information. "In case you decide you want to do it," he said.

I rushed home to check out the websites already running under the Fetisynth banner. There were several XXX brands, ranging from girls fucking machines to lesbian wrestling matches to BDSM-oriented role play complemented by hetero sex. The website the man had told me about wasn't launched yet. Though, from the acts I'd witnessed, I was able to piece together an idea of what I might be in for.

"Why not?" I asked myself, and listed off the reasons why I shouldn't do porn. If I was going to run for political office, it was probably a bad idea. Also, I might piss off my parents. There was risk of venereal disease, but the model application page on Fetisynth's website stated that they required mandatory STI testing prior to a shoot.

I felt comfortable enough with the repercussions that I'd imagined.

My curiosity got the best of me. I made the phone call to set up my first porn shoot.

***

The Fetisynth studio was located in an old warehouse in San Francisco. Once inside, I met a tall blonde woman who looked to be in her early thirties. She introduced herself as Madame Rose. She said that she was a friend of the artist who'd recommended me, and that she was the webmaster for a new website called ToppedBoundBoys.com.

She sat me down and handed me a model release. I glanced it over and signed my name. Then Madame Rose led me to an elevator that shuttled us to a basement-turned-dungeon that Fetisynth had crafted for shooting content. A small crew was there, setting up lights on a semi-enclosed set – something designed to look like a medical office from Hell. There was a lot of chipped paint and fake blood.

My co-star sat in a chair and played with her phone.

"I'm Tiffany," she said.

"David."

She extended her hand. A handshake seemed like too formal of a gesture, considering what we were about to do. But I couldn't think of any other greeting more appropriate for two people meeting for the first time.

Tiffany disrobed while Madame Rose tied me to a chair with rubber hosing. All the while, we engaged in casual conversation. To the people around me, it was a day-to-day experience, so it made sense for an air of normalcy to prevail. It was only in the back of my mind that I kept reminding myself: something new was about to happen. I wasn't a virgin. But I was still lacking that straight-boy rite of passage. My cock had never been inside a pussy.

I had an hour of foreplay, most of which consisted of mild

torture. My favorite part was when Tiffany put down her implements of pain, like whips and electric toys, and nursed my cock with her mouth. With her lips around me, I came to understand how sex work could be a talent. I wished Tiffany all the success in the world.

By the time she rolled a condom down my shaft, the whole act seemed close to natural. We were fucking. It didn't matter that she was a woman. It just felt good.

At the end of the day, my ass was bruised and my jaw was sore from the ball gag Madame Rose had shoved in my mouth. But I looked at the experience as a positive one. The paycheck wasn't bad either.

It wasn't a tough decision, then, when Fetisynth asked me to accompany them to the Napa Valley for a week-long production. One of their original guys had cancelled last minute, and they needed a replacement. School was still a month away, so I had no immediate plans. I told them, "Yes," and packed my bags for the trip.

The cast and crew all met at the Fetisynth studios, and piled into a few extra-large vans for the journey north. As the newest addition, I was given last priority. So I rode in a station wagon with a young woman who had been hired to cook our meals. Her name was Mika. She was an up-and-coming chef at a vegan restaurant in the Sunset District.

Mika and I hit it off. We talked about horror films, sex, and food. She described her kind of vegan culinary style, and nearly convinced me to give up meat. By the time we made it to Napa, we'd formed a clique between just the two of us.

The rest of the week went like clockwork. I woke up early to shower and ready myself for a scene. Then I'd get tied up, beaten, and fucked. After another shower, I'd hang around the kitchen with Mika. We were near inseparable for the latter part of the days. Not that we had any romantic interest. Mika was a full-fledged lesbian, and I was already getting my daily dose of aberrational heterosexuality.

By the end of the week, I'd made a new friend. Plus, the Fetisynth people seemed to like my performances well enough, and said that they'd hire me on a regular basis. I took it all as a sign that I was right where I needed to be.

THE DORM

"HELLO?"

I could feel his throbbing pulse. It was a steady beat, fifteen yards away; a metronome to show the confidence of his every move. His blood flowed calm and steady, as if he had nothing to fear. But I'd already set his death in motion. I'd already found the place where my teeth would rip him apart.

"Earth to David. This is Louis speaking. In English, your native tongue."

The man and his partner – the two in blue uniforms – turned a corner down the hall and...

I breathed, exhaled, and swallowed the abundance of saliva I'd collected on my tongue. I sensed the blurred movement of a figure; an out-of-focus shape, vying for my attention.

"Come on, David. This isn't supposed to be a piece on inanimate objects."

My thoughts came back. So did an awareness of something other than hunger. I managed to curb the beast within me, if only barely.

"Look into the camera and tell me what the fuck is up with your teeth. When did you do that?"

The voice outside my head increased in volume. I tried to focus on the sound. It was familiar, but I couldn't quite place it.

Not until someone put a hand on me and forced my eyes open.

My vision cleared, and I saw my classmate, Louis, standing before me. He stared down the viewfinder of his camcorder, and said, "You take something? Like, pills or..."

"What?" I said, and rubbed my eyes.

"Are you okay?"

The answer was, "No." But I couldn't tell him why. I needed Louis to take me to his dorm room so that I could buy some time and come up with a plan. Because I had no idea what I was supposed to do.

"Sorry," I said. "I was just fucking around."

"Okay." Louis rolled his eyes. "So, like I was saying a minute ago, what did you do to your teeth?"

I brought my hand to my mouth, almost as a reflex. My canines were still elongated and razor sharp at the ends. I pricked my finger, and waved my hand in the air to dissipate the pain.

"Yeah, those," said Louis.

"I don't know," I said. "I was bored, I guess."

"Well, can you take them out? I don't want you to hurt yourself."

"Um. Maybe."

"Maybe what? Remember to repeat the question in the answer, so that I can edit out my own voice."

"Aren't you turning this in tomorrow?" I said. "You're not going to have time to edit anything."

"If you'd fucking cooperate, then maybe I would."

"Fine," I said. "What do you want me to do?"

"Follow me."

***

I heard a melody of hushed voices from behind a metal frame. Louis approached the door and tapped lightly above the handle.

The voices dissipated.

"Open up," said Louis. "It's me."

The door swung inwards to reveal a group of five kids, only one of whom I recognized.

Louis introduced me. "This is David, the guy I was talking about."

"Oh hey," said a boy on the floor. "Louis showed us pictures of your wiener. On the internet." He laughed. "But yeah, it looks good, dude."

"Uh, thanks," I said.

Louis closed the door and went to rummage through the mess under his bed. "I think I have some..." He pulled out a water bottle half-filled with yellow liquid.

"No, no, don't drink that," said a boy who sat atop one of the beds. "I think I pissed in it."

"This is my stuff," said Louis. "You can't just throw your piss wherever you want."

"Sorry. I put it back where I found it."

"You did not find your piss under my bed," said Louis.

"I meant the bottle."

"Uh huh." Louis turned to me. "So the pisser's my roommate, Andrew. This is Ashley." A brunette girl, who sat on the bed, smiled and gave me a little wave. "Casper's on the floor, and these two are Alessandra and Alessandro." He pointed towards the opposite bed. "Yes, it's a coincidence, and yes, they're dating. And yes, I've been trying to get them drunk enough to do whatever it is they do when I'm not watching."

"Louis," said Alessandra. "I'm not having sex in front of you."

"Did I say that?"

Alessandro began to kiss Alessandra's neck. She said, "Babe, stop it. Louis is a perv, and I'm not ending up on 4Chan."

Louis pointed his camera at Alessandra. "You think my work is for some fucking image board? Like, I'm just a fucking troll?"

"I don't think it," said Alessandra. "I know for a fact."

Louis told Alessandra to fuck off, in a playful kind of way, and said, "And we're moving along to..." He scanned the room with his camera and stopped on the boy on the floor. "Casper. Your thoughts on life? Maybe something less ominous?"

"I can handle life," said Casper, who sipped from a bottle of off-brand vodka. "Because I'm living it."

"Beautifully stated."

"I can remember being in the womb," said Casper. "Which is unusual."

"Impossible, actually," said Andrew.

"Why would I make this up?" said Casper. "I was a prenatal prodigy."

"That's not a real thing," said Andrew.

"You're just jealous," said Casper. "Because I had an advanced brain for my age."

"Correct me if I'm wrong," said Louis. "But don't we start counting age once we drop out our momma's pussy?"

"Your age marks how long you've been alive, right?" said Casper.

"Sure," said Andrew. "So wait, how old are you?"

"If I can remember shit from the womb, I was alive and had been for a while." Casper looked at the camera. "Before I dropped out my momma."

"You're against women's reproductive rights?" said Louis. "I mean, if you think you were alive to the extent that you could remember shit, you have to believe it's murder for your mom to take you out with a coat hanger."

"Are we really talking about this?" said Alessandra. She sounded almost angry.

I took a seat in a computer chair, stationed at a small desk in the corner of the room. It seemed that Louis had forgotten about me. So I seized the moment to reflect on what had happened – what I'd done and what I'd become.

Daniel said something before the bathroom; before you killed him. That he would clear up our past. He didn't clear up anything, right?

Maybe he's become a figment of his own imagination. Maybe I've become a part of it too.

What if it's not his imagination?

He's not a fucking vampire.

Then how do you explain the past few days? Your new set of teeth?

It was just a fantasy. Teenage bullshit. Because we were into that band.

THE BAND

DANIEL AND I FIRST DEVELOPED OUR TASTE FOR music in middle school. Like a lot of kids with Y chromosomes, we were into heavy metal. It was probably Metallica, Korn, or some other band with a lot of airplay that first got us into distorted guitars and heavy drums. But Daniel was the first, between us, to discover something faster and darker.

He said that he was watching TV when he came across a daytime documentary special. The show was about a Norwegian band that played a style of music called black metal. Supposedly, the musicians had set fire to a number of churches across the country. It had something to do with their stance on religion in their culture.

Daniel was curious, and wanted to know more. So he went to the internet to sort it all out. What he found, he said, garnered my immediate attention.

He burst through my bedroom door one day after school, and said, "You have to hear this."

I tried to keep up with him as he sprinted back across the street. But Daniel was already at the computer, headphones strapped to his ears, when I entered his room. He handed me a separate pair of headphones that he'd jacked into his computer speakers.

"Ready?" he asked.

I put on the headphones, and waited for the noise. Suddenly, my ears were pummeled by the sound of blast-beat drums and speed-picked guitars. Seconds later, a high-pitched voice shrieked phrases of indecipherable meaning. It sounded like the battle cry of a mythic beast or warrior. By the end of the song, I felt my heart race, like I was ready for a battle of my own.

"What is this?" I asked.

Daniel said, "Black metal," and told me that the music carried a sort of ideology along with it.

Like the daytime documentary had claimed, many black metal bands held a certain anti-Christian stance. But Daniel and I continued our online research, and found a wealth of other concepts explored within the genre. The lyrical content and album artwork often stemmed from pagan mythology. Or just pure fantasy. Whatever the emphasis, violent opposition to the mainstream seemed like a common thread.

Daniel and I believed that we'd stumbled upon something profound. The absence of true conflict in our town left us with little to rebel against. So we latched on to a kind of music founded in rebellion. We felt a visceral connection with the sound, and attempted to embrace the lifestyle. At least, as far as we understood it.

Daniel came up with the idea to start a band. He'd been practicing screaming into pillows when our parents weren't home, so he appointed himself as our vocalist. I'd already picked up the guitar a year prior. So I felt ready to volunteer myself as an axe-yielding member of the band. All we needed was a drummer and a bass player.

We asked the only kid at school we knew to own a drum kit. His name was Jesse Silverstein. He was the son of a jazz pianist and feminist author. He didn't share our enthusiasm for extreme metal, but his parents urged him to join the group in order to diversify his talents. The approval of authority figures put us off at first, but the practice space Jesse's parents offered up was too good to pass over.

The last addition to the band was Henry Feist, a recent transfer student to our middle school. We befriended him because he wore a lot of black t-shirts. It seemed like the only way to determine who shared our *dark* sensibility. In any case, Henry was into heavy music, and his dad owned a bass. He commandeered the instrument and joined us.

We practiced for about a year before we gained the confidence to present our music in front of an audience. During that time, Daniel carefully crafted a performance alter ego to front the band. While the rest of us worked to build instrumental compositions, Daniel studied other bands in order to figure out what he had to say. It was a form of plagiarism, sure. But I couldn't blame him. My guitar riffs weren't exactly original.

Daniel discovered a European black metal band called Vampinokturne, an operatic four-piece who portrayed themselves as vampires. Members of the band were rumored to have murdered people for their blood. No evidence surfaced to substantiate the claims. But Daniel became fascinated by the idea that they might have existed as something other than human.

He adopted Vampinokturne's lyrical themes of blood-lust and immortality. Then he started to complain about sunlight, and wore makeup to emphasize his pale skin and the ideals of eternal youth.

During our first show, Daniel emptied a half-bottle of pig's blood into his mouth and spit it out at the audience. It wasn't the most original example of shock-rock theatrics, but for a fourteen-year-old kid, it came off as hardcore. If our band sucked, it didn't matter. People heard about Daniel's antics, and wanted to see them up close.

While Daniel helped our band to become a small town phenomenon, I began to experience another part of him. We returned from a show one night to unload our gear at Jesse's place, and drink a case of beer we'd stolen from his parents. Henry passed out shortly after midnight. Jesse went to bed. Daniel and I were left alone together.

We were drunk and laughing. Daniel kept telling me that he wanted to bite my neck. At first, I played it off like he was joking. Then I drank more beer, and no longer cared whether or not he tried. "Okay," I said. "I guess you can do it."

Daniel looked excited. He approached my skin, and then stopped and sort of inhaled with his mouth. It was like he was smelling me. I didn't know if he was just playing, or whether he was actually building up the courage to bite into me. His lips grazed my neck, and without the sharpness of his teeth.

I couldn't figure out what was happening at first. But I didn't pull away. In fact, I welcomed his touch, and what felt like his affection.

Daniel stopped nursing my neck, and brought his face up close to mine. We sat in a moment of apprehension. I didn't know if my desire had been waiting all along, or if it first appeared in a cosmic spark.

Sure, his face had crossed my mind some nights when I'd jerked off. And I'd compared his body to boys at school when I'd tried to think of who was "hot." But he was my brother, in some way, and always seemed off-limits. Until his mouth was next to mine, and I wanted so much of him inside me.

I wasn't sure who made it happen, but our lips came together. We gnawed at each other's mouths, and drank the spit that flowed from our tongues. It felt like our first everything. And I cherished it.

STUDENT FILMS

"COME ON, SLEEPY HEAD," SAID LOUIS. "I HAVEN'T even started with you yet."

I removed my face from my hands, and sat up.

Louis crouched before me. His camera was still on. "I dragged you all the way down here. So I'm not letting you nod off before I get something good."

"I don't think I'm in the mood for what you want," I said.

"Wait," said Louis. "What did you do with your teeth?"

"What do you mean?"

"The fangs," said Louis. "The big fucking chompers you were showing off in the hall. When did you take them out?"

I ran my tongue across the top row of my teeth, and realized that they'd returned to normal. "I took them out," I said, and knew that I sounded unsure.

Louis was intrigued. "Show me how you do it."

"No."

"Why not?"

"Because..." My mouth hung open for an excessive amount of time. I decided on a truth that I didn't quite believe was real. Because everything else I could imagine was equally implausible. "I'm a vampire."

"Okay," said Louis. "That's not exactly what I was going for.

But roll with it."

I squinted my eyes. "What do you want me to say?"

"David," said Louis. "If you're going to make shit up, you have to make more shit up. That's how it works." His voice became sultry. "Just make it good."

"I just told you that I'm a vampire," I said. "Like, the kind that drinks people's blood. I can't show my fangs because..." I tried to piece together the puzzle I'd been given. "They only appear when I'm about to kill someone."

"But I just saw your fangs a few minutes ago," said Louis. He swung the camera all around him. "I don't see any dead bodies."

"I stopped myself," I said, and leaned back in the chair.

"So bring them back," said Louis. "Kill..." He pointed the camera to the opposite side of the room. "...Andrew."

Andrew broke from his conversation with one of the other students. "What?"

"David wants to prove that he's a vampire," said Louis. "So I volunteered you for an experiment."

"What do I have to do?" said Andrew.

Louis shrugged. "I guess you don't have to do anything."

"Then what's he going to do to me?" said Andrew.

Louis shoved the camera in my face, like he expected me to answer.

"Nothing," I said. "I have nothing to prove."

"You have a lot to prove," said Louis, under his breath. "Just come over here." He patted a spot on the bed next to Andrew. "Have a seat. Get comfortable. You're a guest in my home."

I leaned back in the computer chair, stretched out my legs, and provoked Louis with a smile. "And look, I've made myself at home."

Louis' face turned sour. "Yeah, well that's my fucking chair, and I want you out of it." He kicked playfully at my shins. "Come on. Up, up!"

"Okay, okay." I sat down on the bed, next to Andrew. "Happy?"

"We'll see," said Louis.

"I'm out of here," said Alessandra, who took her boyfriend by the wrist.

"Really?" said Louis. "This could be good."

"I don't think so," said Alessandra. Alessandro seemed to agree.

"Okay. Bye? Thanks for drinking my beer?" Louis lifted his middle finger as the couple slipped out the door.

"Adios," said Casper, and he toasted them goodbye.

The door clicked shut. Louis said, to no one in particular, "Why the fuck was she even here?"

No one answered.

"I have a quick question about the vampire thing," said Andrew, who raised his hand slightly.

"Yeah," said Louis. "We're getting to that." He kept the camera pointed at me. "So how does this work? When you usually... what would you say? Eat someone?"

"I guess so."

"Okay," said Louis. "So when you eat a person, do you start at the neck like we'd assume? Or is there a better place to, um, latch on?"

I was uncomfortable at the reality of our conversation – at what Louis had assumed was just a joke. But I continued on, because I didn't know what else to do. "It's like you said. I bite at the neck."

Casper laughed. Ashley put a finger to her mouth. "Let him finish," she said. I looked at her, and tried to understand her reason for defending me.

"How about you take a little bite out of Andrew," said Louis.

"Fuck off," said Andrew.

"Andrew," said Louis, "he's not a vampire. This is pretend. Just let him nuzzle your neck for fuck's sake."

"I'm not gay," said Andrew. He turned to me, and said, "No offense."

"This isn't about sex," said Louis. "I'm making a movie. Can you play the victim for one fucking minute? Please?"

"Fine," said Andrew, and his voice was something bitter. "Do you want me to act surprised? What do you want me to do?"

"Whatever you would do if someone bit you," said Louis. "Okay. Action!"

"This isn't a good idea," I said.

"Just do it," said Louis.

I set my eyes on the skin of Andrew's neck. It seemed so easy. All I had to do was pretend to bite him. Louis would be happy, and he'd stop with his movie. I could sit and think. All I wanted was some time to figure things out.

But as I stared at Andrew's flesh, I felt a hunger overcome me. His arteries emerged, like a pulsing feast ripe for the taking. I descended into a primitive state; became ravenous.

I placed my mouth over Andrew's neck. There was no resistance. I clamped down with my jaw, and rushed my emerging fangs into his carotid.

Andrew let out a yelp.

"Good," said Louis. "But just a little bit more of a reaction." Andrew screamed, and Louis said, "That's better."

Andrew amplified his struggle. He hit me wherever he could, and yelled, "Get him off me! Get him the fuck off me!"

I felt a small tug at my back. Moments later, a force ripped me from my place at Andrew's neck and sent me to the floor. My vision blurred. I tried to shake off the trauma. As I regained my physical orientation, a shred of intellect came along with it. The hunger was still inside me. But I'd become aware of my actions, and before they'd taken place.

There was Casper, above me. He appeared to have thrown me to the ground. Andrew was still on the bed, clutching his neck, as if he could stop the blood from spilling out his wound. I heard a girl's whimper from my right-hand side, and saw Ashley with her back pressed against the wall. Behind me, there was Louis, retreating in his step. He still held the camera; still recorded everything.

I brought myself to my knees in the center of the room. Hushed cries surged from all around me. The students slowly distanced themselves. But I could sense the panic in their sweat and smell it on their tears.

Andrew cried softly. "Call someone. I'm fucking dying." He shivered, and let more of himself pour on to the bed.

I didn't want to harm anyone. But my hunger was still strong. I wiped my mouth and licked the remaining blood from my hand, and then rose to my feet. "I'm sorry," I said, but no one would reply. I forced my way to the door and let myself out, and tried my best to stay quiet.

Out in the hall, I felt a rush of air come up behind me. A black cloth wrapped around my face. I tried to call out, but felt a blow delivered to my head. My body sank, and my mind descended into darkness.

SEX AND VIOLENCE

I WOKE UP AND FELT A HEADACHE COME ON strong. It was the morning after our first kiss. Daniel was still asleep beside me. I put a hand on him and shook him. He slowly woke and rubbed his eyes.

We didn't talk about what happened. In fact, we barely spoke at all.

My mother picked us up from Jesse's place and drove us home. The whole ride was spent in silence. Daniel wouldn't even look at me. I wasn't ashamed of what we'd done. I only feared that Daniel felt otherwise.

I sat alone in my room for the rest of the day, and browsed Daniel's Livejournal. At first, I looked for any mention of my name; any clue that might reveal what he thought of me. Then I stared at his pictures and jerked off, and imagined my mouth on him again.

We returned to school, and eased back into our old routine. It seemed like our night at Jesse's had been a dream, and one I'd have to forget.

But halfway through the day, Daniel and I walked together through the hall of the east science wing, on our way from one class to another. My left hand hung limp by my side. I felt a light pull at my fingertips, and saw that Daniel's hand grasped at mine. My palm slid into his, and we continued to walk, but with smiles on our faces.

Then we heard a voice, like a catcall from behind us. I wasn't able to make out the words. But I looked, and saw a group of boys I recognized from the school's football team. The boys laughed and whispered to each other, and offered glances in our direction.

I broke away from Daniel's grip, and told him that we should hurry to class or we'd be late. But Daniel pulled me back and pressed me against the nearest locker. Then he brought his lips to mine. Daniel pushed his tongue inside my mouth, and stretched his jaw to emphasize every motion. It was as if he got off by putting us on display.

I had always known Daniel to want attention, especially for what people pointed out in him as different. He took such qualities as a sign of his superiority, and often sought to punish those below him – those who'd disagree.

One of the football players threw a bottle of soda at us. It hit the locker next to my head, and exploded cola across my face. I was pissed, but knew that Daniel had wanted it to happen. He'd wanted an excuse.

He sprinted down the hall. The boys stood frozen, like they couldn't believe what was coming for them. Daniel slammed his forehead into the boy he reached first. I heard the crunch of a broken nose. The remaining boys tackled Daniel to the ground.

I rushed towards the commotion, threw my fists, and blindly fished for the impact of flesh and bone. But I was soon met with an elbow to the cheek and a shove to the floor. I remained there on my back, blocking blows until campus security arrived to break up the fight. Within half an hour, everyone involved was suspended from school.

***

Daniel and I were sent home, and placed in my mother's care. She was the only one of our parents who had the day off from work.

"So you two were what?" said my mother, when Daniel and I were alone with her on the couch. "Making out at school? With each other?"

Daniel and I exchanged glances in hopes that the other might know how to respond.

"I don't get it," said my mother. "Is this some kind of a stunt? You two are practically brothers."

"But we're not," I said. "Not really."

My mother took a long pause. "Don't you like girls?"

"Aren't we in trouble for fighting?" said Daniel. "That's why we got suspended."

"Sure," said my mother. "I'm just trying to get to the root of the problem. You were in a fight because..."

"They threw a bottle at us," I said.

"Why would they do that?" said my mother.

"Because they're bigot-fucking-football-nazis!" said Daniel.

"Daniel!" said my mother. "You two were making out."

"You've been fucking my dad for how many years now?" said Daniel. "Why is it such a big deal for me to kiss David?"

"It wasn't even the first time," I said.

"What?" said my mother.

"Mom, we didn't do anything wrong."

"You're suspended from school, aren't you? That means something is wrong. And I didn't know about all this kissing, so apparently I have no idea what my children are up to."

"I'm not your kid," said Daniel.

"I raised you for six years," said my mother, "and you're still over here all the time."

"Because we're friends," I said.

"Friends don't make out with each other," said my mother.

"Then we're more than friends," I said.

"What is that supposed to mean?" asked my mother.

I looked to Daniel, and then to the floor. "Maybe I like him."

"Are you telling me, David," said my mother, "that you're gay? It sounds like that's what you're telling me."

I shrugged, and so did Daniel. He said, "Maybe a little bit."

My mother closed her eyes and took several deep breaths. "What am I supposed to tell your fathers?"

"That we have the next week off of school?" I said. My mother walked away, and with her hands up in the air.

***

That night, after dinner, Mr. Brion came into my bedroom. He handed me a brown paper bag full of magazines and a bookmarked Bible. "These might help," he said. "With what you've been going through."

I opened the bag when he was gone. It held a collection of hetero-pornography dating back to the 1970's. Some of the porn was amusing, but I felt more embarrassed than aroused. The Bible wasn't even worth looking at. I threw it in the trash can next to my desk.

My sexual fulfillment didn't come until later. Daniel appeared outside my window shortly before midnight. He tapped at the glass until I let him in. Then he pushed me on to the bed and bit my lip. He ripped off what little clothing I had on, and I helped as he removed his own. When we were skin on skin, he straddled my chest and waved his cock at my lips.

"Oh my God," I tried to say, as I gagged, sucked, and swallowed him.

INTERNMENT

MY HEAD HUNG FORWARD LIKE A ROTTING APPLE from a tree branch. If gravity had its way, I would have fallen face first to the floor. But something held me back. I tried to lurch forward, but my arms remained behind me, strapped to the chair I was sitting in.

A dull ache spread from the back of my skull and infected my swollen skin. My bones suffered, and fatigue set into every muscle. A dense fabric stretched across my face. The cloth reached down, past my nose and mouth, and stifled my every breath.

Where am I?

The other voice in me was silent – retreated into the corner of my mind for fear of being discovered.

The last thing I remembered was leaving Louis' room, a pain, and then darkness.

A creak wailed in the distance, and sounded like an ungreased hinge. The noise stretched my nerves taut, like wire beneath my skin. My ears remained open and became king over all my other senses. They peaked in distortion at the patter of approaching footsteps.

In an instant, all was calm. Not a sound could be heard. No sense of motion could be felt in the still, dead air. I imagined myself alone, isolated in the eye of a storm. The only precipitation dripped from my eyes and clung to my cheeks like glass. When the cloth hood was ripped from my head, I stared up, expecting a blizzard embodied as a supernatural wraith. But there was only a man.

He crouched, so that his eyes were level with mine, and said, "Boo!"

I slammed back in the chair, and sprayed piss down my leg. The man broke into laughter while I whimpered aloud in frightened catharsis.

He eyed the growing stain on my pants. "At least you didn't shit yourself."

I heard another set of footsteps, and another voice – a woman's. "Leave the boy alone," she said. "He's been through enough."

The woman approached and bent down before me. "I'm Astrid," she said. "You must be David."

I found the strength to nod.

"I'm sorry for the way you've been treated," said Astrid. "But we needed to be careful. Considering what you did to Daniel."

How does she know Daniel?

"You've no doubt noticed some changes," said Astrid. "Since he bit you. Under different circumstances, we'd have brought you here as a welcoming. But you tried to kill my friend." She spoke again, as if to correct herself. "Our friend."

"Some kind of friend," said the man behind her.

"Ian, please," said Astrid.

The man, Ian, rolled his eyes and retreated to the furthest wall.

Astrid looked back to me. "First, I want to know," she said. "What do you believe has happened to you?"

I let my mouth separate. But my words were stuck inside, trembling beneath my throat.

"I'll make it easier for you," said Astrid. "Do you know what you've become?"

I nodded, because I felt almost certain.

"So it can't be such a giant step to assume that we, too, are..."

I found my voice, and finished Astrid's sentence for her. "Vampires." The word echoed in my head. It was a final confirmation of my life and mythology merged into one.

"Good," said Astrid. She smiled and looked to Ian.

"What?" said Ian. "You don't think Hitler knew he was a Jew?"

"Understand our concern," said Astrid. "You are one of us. But we need to know that you accept it."

I gulped down a breath of dry air, and gave her another nod.

"Okay," said Astrid, and she stood to move behind me. "I'm going to assume that what happened with Daniel was a result of fear." She began to untie my hands.

"Astrid," said Ian. He approached and bore his fangs; made a sound, like a growl, as if he'd meant to warn me.

Astrid loosened another strand of rope. "Luckily, you didn't know what you were doing, and our friend is still alive." The twine fell from my wrists. Astrid brought her mouth up to my ear. "But if you ever try to hurt him again..."

The door to the room burst open, and Daniel came storming through. He appeared alive and healthy. Resurrected to his vibrant form. My eyes locked with his, and I felt somehow safe for the first time since I'd arrived.

"We've only had him for the night," said Astrid to Daniel. "I had to make sure he wouldn't harm you."

Daniel looked to my wrists and to the pattern of rope still burned into my skin. "Thank you," he said. "Can I have a moment alone with him?"

"Daniel," said Ian. "He shoved a piece of metal through your chest."

"And we've all done much worse," said Daniel. "Leave us alone."

Ian gave me a look, like he meant to hurt me, and exited the room. Astrid followed.

Once they'd gone and shut the door behind them, Daniel approached me without hesitation. He knelt at my feet and looked me over. "All that's happened is behind us now," he said, and broke into a contagious smile.

My shell of fear began to crack. "How are you alive?"

Daniel slowly stood. "You know." He embraced me, and a tear rolled down my cheek. "I gave you a gift, David."

"Yeah?" I said. "You wrapped it in *some* package."

DISAPPEARANCE

DANIEL AND I DECIDED TO DECREASE OUR public displays of affection at school. We'd received lectures about our lifestyle from our parents, counselors, and even a local youth pastor that my mother had arranged for us to see. Given the dirty looks we still received from the football team at school, it just seemed like a good idea to take it easy during the day. To save the black eyes and bruises. Besides, the energy was better spent at home.

At school, I took on the role of an academic drone. But at night, when I was alone with Daniel, I felt like a fucking porn star.

And even though my extracurricular activities were largely devoted to Daniel's body, I still found time and energy to contribute to our band. To my surprise, it started to pay off.

Before the year was through, we recorded our first EP. Our sound had begun to achieve a distinguishing quality, and our performance had become tighter and more aggressive. We managed to attract the attention of a Seattle-based death metal band called Sacrificial Slaughter. They needed a supporting act for their tour and asked us to fill the spot. We agreed to open the string of shows they'd booked throughout Washington, Oregon, and California.

Daniel threw himself across a cramped stage on the first night of tour, and just as I flailed my guitar to the rhythm of some discordant verse. He hit my instrument, snapped off a piece of wood, and ripped a two-inch gash in the side of his scalp. I stopped playing for a few measures to see if he was okay. Daniel grabbed my throat and screamed for me to keep going. He rubbed the blood from his wound across the body of my guitar and gave me a kiss that felt like he was trying to tear my mouth off. The energy from that moment catapulted us into a frenzy that continued throughout the tour.

The kids who came out each night stood still during our first few songs, as if confused. Our seizure-emulating movements were more akin to punk and hardcore bands than to the steady headbanging associated with death and black metal. Combined with Daniel's overt homoeroticism, it seemed like no one knew how to react. That is, until Daniel forced them to. He'd grab someone from the audience – whoever stood closest – and throw him across the room. Some nights, he'd try to bite a patron's neck, or knock him to the floor and spit in his face.

One night, things got out of hand.

We were playing somewhere in the outskirts of Eugene, Oregon, to an audience of pirate punks, metal heads, and a small group of militant-looking skinheads. The skins took notice to Daniel's gestures, like fellating the mic in front of my crotch, and came up to the stage to flip us off, hurl insults, and throw punches any time one of us came close enough.

Daniel took a fist to the back of his calf, and fell to one knee. So he grabbed the mic and swung it into the nearest skin's face. The rest of them rushed the stage and tried to obliterate our band.

Those of us with instruments turned them into makeshift

weapons. Jesse swung pieces of his drum kit and used the stands as spears. Henry and I tried to deal as much damage as we could with our guitars, and without breaking them. Daniel only had his hands and feet to fight with.

There were enough anarchists, crust punks, and metal heads among the crowd who seemed to like our band. The skins were soon outnumbered and kicked to the street by a small mob. The downside was that, in the midst of the brawl, someone had called the cops. The show was shut down, and the crowd told to disband. We were left outside the club, nursing our wounds with the guys from Sacrificial Slaughter.

Daniel held the side of his head with a blood-crusted shirt. He turned to the Roger, the frontman for Sacrificial Slaughter. "Sorry we ruined the gig for you guys."

"It's all good. You killed it, so whatever."

"If you only knew how many shows skins have fucked up around here," said Aaron, the drummer for Sacrificial Slaughter. "About time that they were showed the fucking door."

"You play here a lot?" I asked.

Aaron shook his head. "Not really. I just recognize some of those guys from a few years back. When I used to live in Eugene."

"Oh shit," said Roger. "Are those the skins you were telling me about from the Vampinokturne show?"

"Yeah, I think so," said Aaron. "Fucking nazis."

"Wait," I said. "You've seen Vampinokturne?"

"They came through here on their last US tour."

"When was that?" said Daniel, with a mix of excitement and disappointment.

"Not sure exactly," said Aaron. "I was still living here, so it must have been about three years ago."

"I don't care how many skinheads showed up," said Daniel. "I would have killed to see that show."

"In case you couldn't tell," I said. "They're kind of our favorite band."

Roger laughed. "You're into that vampire act, huh?"

"Act or not," said Daniel. "They slay."

"They're alright," said Aaron. "But come on. When I rolled out to that show, it was like a LARPing match. Fuck the skins. I was more likely to be hit by a twelve-sided dice."

"Don't hate on the D&D kids," I said, and laughed. "Henry's all about it."

"Hey!" shouted Henry, from inside the van. "It's nothing to be ashamed of."

Roger peered through the van's grimy window. "Don't worry. I was into dumber shit than you at your age."

"You're what?" said Daniel. "Four years older than us?"

"I'm twenty-two," said Roger.

"Okay. Six years," said Daniel. "So what does your mature ass want to do tonight now that we're out of a show?"

"I know something you kids will love," said Aaron.

"What?" I asked.

"There's an urban legend out here," said Aaron. "When I was growing up, there was this family that lived about thirty minutes outside the city, in house that looked like a barn. They mostly kept to themselves. Probably farmed their own food, or whatever. For some reason, there were always rumors going around."

"So..." I didn't see how Aaron's story had anything to do with the night's activities.

"So," said Aaron, "the rumor I heard most was that this family was actually a clan of fucking vampires. Most people wouldn't go near the place."

Daniel and I started to laugh. “You just gave us shit for liking Vampinokturne,” I said. “And you’re going to tell me there’s a bunch of real-life vampires held up in a barn?”

Aaron gave us a big, toothy grin. “Why don’t we have a look?”

“Fuck all of you,” said Roger. “I’m going to find a bar. You can call me when we’re leaving.”

Aaron turned to Daniel and me. “So what do you say?”

“Sure,” said Daniel. It sounded like there was a hint of curiosity tucked beneath his sarcasm. “Let’s go look at a barn.”

***

We drove for about thirty minutes. Daniel, Henry, and I all packed into the back of the Sacrificial Slaughter tour van. Aaron took the wheel. The city lights of Eugene faded, and we found ourselves somewhere between the suburbs and the middle of nowhere.

Soon enough, we came across a large, barn-shaped house, just as Aaron had described. He parked the van under a canopy of trees, and we all jumped out.

“We should be safe from here,” said Aaron.

“Stop,” I said.

“I’m serious,” said Aaron. “Anyone goes missing around here, guess who gets the blame?”

“So what?” said Henry. “We’re just supposed to look at it?”

Aaron crossed his arms. “I’m not saying they’re vampires. But whoever lives in there... They don’t want people around for a reason.”

“So why’d you even take us out here?” I said.

“It’s kind of like a dare,” said Aaron.

“What is?” asked Henry.

“We used to do it as kids,” said Aaron. “A bunch of us would get together. Hide in the trees. We'd dare each other to go up to the house. Whoever went the farthest, peaked in the windows or whatever, we'd all give him a dollar."

"I'm sure that was exhilarating when you were, like, ten," I said. "But there's no way I'm going to doorbell ditch some rednecks in the middle of the night."

"I'll do it," said Daniel.

My response was immediate, and like an instinctive cry of confusion. "What? Why?"

Daniel shrugged, just as he had when he'd first agreed for us to go on the expedition. "We're already here," he said. "And... Why not?"

"Exactly," said Aaron. "Let's make it interesting. See that small light coming off the top of the roof?"

We looked at what appeared to be an orange glow emanating off the top, left slant of the roof.

"Yeah, I see it," said Henry, and he seemed to speak for all of us.

"It's a window," said Aaron. "A sunroof or something. The only kid I know who climbed up there and looked inside... He disappeared a few days later. No one's seen him since. True story."

"Bullshit," I said.

"I'm not saying it had anything to do with the house," said Aaron. "But what if it did?"

"So you want me to go on the roof?" said Daniel. "Is that it?"

I tried to intervene. "Don't be an asshole. Someone lives there."

"I'm not going to fuck anything up," said Daniel. "I'm just going to climb up there and look in the window. And Aaron will suck my dick."

"Nothing passes my lips that I don't chew and swallow," said Aaron. "So if you want to take your chances."

"Then what's in it for me?" said Daniel. "I'm going to need more than a dollar."

"I'll suck your dick not to do it," I said.

Aaron rolled his eyes. "You'll blow him regardless." He had a point. "But for you, Daniel, if you climb up there and flash this little fucker..." Aaron removed a mini-mag light from his key chain and slid it into Daniel's palm. "So we can see you. I'll buy you dinner for the rest of tour."

"Deal," said Daniel.

"But keep it under five bucks a meal," said Aaron.

"Fuck you," said Daniel. "But still a deal."

"What if you get caught?" I said.

"I'll run," said Daniel. "You can meet me halfway with the van." Daniel turned to Aaron, as if to consolidate the plan. "Cool?"

"Yeah, dude. I got your back," said Aaron.

Daniel took off, and raced across a grassy slope that separated us from the barn-house. His figure approached the structure. I held my breath as he disappeared along the black panels that made up the house; tried to search for his movement in the shadows.

"Wait," I said. "How is he supposed to even get on to the roof?"

Aaron shrugged. "The kid I told you about, he used a ladder he found behind the house. If it's still out there, Daniel will find it."

"That was how long ago?" I said. "What if it's not there?"

"Then maybe Daniel won't make it," said Aaron. "I don't know. What are you so worried about?" The question caught me off guard. I was worried. Not about vampires, because I didn't believe that they existed at the time. But as I lost site of Daniel, I felt as though he had disappeared altogether. A warning emerged from my subconscious. It was like a current of knowledge had escaped from inside my brain. I couldn't have known it back then – the string of events that would come from Daniel's response to a simple dare. Still, something inside me screamed.

"I'm not worried," I said, because I didn't want to come off like a clingy, faggot boyfriend. "I just don't think it's the best idea for Daniel to try and scale the side of a house shortly after being hit in the head, repeatedly, by some skinhead crew."

Aaron seemed taken aback. Not by what I said, but by the catty undertone I had delivered it with. I knew I had been compensating for some elusive fear that had taken me over. But I felt better for it. Like I'd been laughing at a funeral.

Aaron scrunched his brow. "Maybe you're right," he said. "You think he might have a concussion?" Aaron jumped into the driver's seat of the van, and pushed his keys into the ignition.

"Look," said Henry, pointing his finger. We all gazed at the small, blinking light atop the massive barn-house.

"That's Daniel, right?" said Henry.

"Fucker actually got on to the roof," said Aaron. He smirked at me. "See, everything's okay. Your little Daniel is all safe and sound."

"Yeah," I said. But as soon as I'd said the word, I heard a distant crash, followed by the patter of feet on shingles. In an instant, we all knew something had happened to Daniel.

"Fuck," said Aaron, under his breath.

The van roared to life, and we were off towards the barn-house with increasing speed. Aaron flicked on the headlights. I could barely see a crouched figure at the base of the structure.

The figure stood and sprinted towards us, and just as a giant door opened at the front of the house.

I wrenched the door open on the side of the van. Aaron eased into the brakes.

"What happened?" Aaron craned his neck back to see Daniel jump into the van.

"Uh, uh..." Daniel was out of breath, and appeared shaken up. I pulled him into the back seat and wrapped my arms around him.

Henry laughed. "They look pissed," he said, and pointed towards the silhouettes standing in the doorway of the barn-house.

Daniel kept blinking, and his eyes stayed shut for longer than they were open. I asked him if he was okay. He looked at me, and then out the window. "Yeah," said Daniel, and he attempted to smile. "I'm fine. Just tripped."

"What, on the roof?" said Aaron.

Daniel nodded and forced a grin. I was the only one close enough to see his lip quiver; to feel his hand reach for mine and grip it tightly. But I didn't say a word. I only listened as Daniel explained his brief stint as a roof-scaling trespasser.

"I found a ladder on the ground," said Daniel, as he looked behind him, at the darkened rural landscape and the building we left behind. "That's how I got up there."

"See," said Aaron, to me. "I told you he'd find his way."

"Did you see them?" said Henry. "Did they look like vampires?"

Daniel gave Henry a look like the boy was some kind of stupid. Then he told us about how he'd crept across the roof and peered down at a family of three – a woman and two men. They'd been eating dinner while he watched. He explained how he fumbled for the flashlight to alert us of his position. That's when he slipped, slid a few feet, and made a whole racket of noise. He'd jumped down the ladder as fast as he could. The rest was as we'd seen it happen.

Aaron laughed, Henry looked disappointed, and I awaited the chance for Daniel to tell me what had really happened. But the tour went on, and he never said another word about it. Never even took Aaron up on the free meals. So I came to believe that his story was true, and that there was nothing more to talk about.

Several weeks later, when Daniel disappeared from my life, it never crossed my mind that a barn in the middle of Oregon had anything to do with it. I had no clues to give the police and no answers to mend my broken heart.

APOLOGIES ARE DANGEROUS

I ROSE FROM THE SMALL, WOODEN CHAIR AND followed Daniel out of the room. My captors, Astrid and Ian, lurked in the hallway outside – a dark tunnel that disappeared in both directions. Light trickled from a fluorescent panel on the ceiling. It cast top-heavy shadows that darkened the crevices in our faces. From where I stood, it appeared that the eyes of those around me had been hollowed out.

I stepped behind Daniel, as if he might protect me from the others.

"So that's it then?" said Ian. His words sounded less like a question and more like a sarcastic indictment against me.

Daniel ignored him and pressed a button on the wall. Several moments later, a set of steel doors opened, and Daniel stepped on to an elevator. I shuffled in beside him and waited to be whisked away.

"We'll see you tomorrow," said Daniel, and with no time for a response. The doors came together, and we began our ascent. We arrived at the top floor, in the middle of Daniel's apartment.

"You keep that place in your basement?" I said, and tried to imagine what other needs he might have for an in-house interrogation room.

"I couldn't keep it up here," he said. "Doesn't really fit the décor."

I couldn't tell whether he'd meant for me to laugh. If so, my body hadn't relaxed enough for it to be possible. I kept my head down, hesitant to make myself at home in the place where I'd nearly murdered my host.

When I glanced up, Daniel was gone.

"In here!" he shouted from another room.

I moved across the marble floor, in attempt to follow his voice, and ended up in a bedroom. Daniel emerged from the closet. He threw me a pair of jeans.

"Try these on," he said, and shifted his eyes to my waist.

I looked at the urine stain on my crotch, and kicked off my pants. My underwear went along with them.

I was met by a hint of unusual embarrassment. I'd become more than accustomed to baring my skin. But there was a lingering notion that I'd done something wrong. Or that I'd assumed a familiarity that no longer existed. The years of separation had erased the comfort I used to have around Daniel.

It was too late to do anything about it. My ass was already in full view, and I couldn't help but notice that Daniel had taken attention. His eyes lingered on my naked skin. I waited a moment longer to slip into his jeans.

"So you want to have a talk?" said Daniel. He removed his shoes and fell on to the bed with his hands behind his head. It was like he was putting on a show; pretending that nothing was wrong, so that I might be more at ease.

I shrugged.

"Sit," he said.

I obeyed, and placed myself on the corner of his mattress. My body was stiff and I stared at the floor. Daniel moved to sit beside me.

“David,” he said, and his voice shrunk in volume. “It’s important to me that this transition be as comfortable for you as possible. I just hoped that I could skip the part that’s... uncomfortable for me.”

Daniel’s jaw tightened. I could only imagine that he was caught in the moment that must occur before one delivers an explanation for abandoning a friend. Even if I was projecting, I allowed him time to soak in what I hoped was a sea of guilt.

Does he even know what I went through when he left?

Of course not. He never even tried to contact you.

Does he really think he can fix it all by turning me into a monster?

Don’t forget sending his friends to kidnap you.

Whatever he says, I’m leaving. He can’t stop me. I’ll rip his fucking head off. I don’t care if it grows back.

I couldn’t say any of it aloud. And I wouldn’t want him to hear it. Not with my body still awash in the residue of fear and degradation. He’d see my outrage for what it was: a blanket to hide old wounds, newly salted.

“I’m sorry,” said Daniel. “I didn’t mean for things to turn out the way they did.” He paused. “You remember the last time we toured? I guess it was the only time. But you remember, right?”

I nodded.

“There was that night when – I don’t remember his name, but the drummer from Sacrificial Slaughter – took us to a house in the middle of nowhere. Said vampires lived there. I don’t expect you to remember, but he dared me to go up on the roof.”

“I remember,” I said. “Your hands were trembling when you

got back in the van."

"Yeah?"

"Yeah."

"I saw them," said Daniel. "Astrid, Ian, and another vampire. I looked through the window, and saw them feasting on some woman. Saw them drink her blood. I'd never seen anything like that before. Not in real life."

"Why didn't you tell me?" I asked.

"I was going to," said Daniel. "But I was afraid you wouldn't believe me. What if it was some sort of tourist trick? I had to find out for sure. All my petty dreams and emulations of this thing, this creature... to find out that it was actually real. God, I wanted it more than anything in the world."

It hurt me all the more to know that his want had eclipsed me. "Why couldn't I have known too? Why just leave?"

"I didn't just leave. That's why it took me the rest of tour, and more, to make a decision. Even when I did, I meant to come back for you."

I waited for the inevitable.

"But they needed me, David. I came to them with the want to be a vampire. Astrid, Ian... They never thought that someone would want to be like them. They'd been holed up in that place, scared of the rest of the world, for longer than they'd like to admit. They thought they'd be hunted down if they went out in the open."

"So what?" I said.

"I became, I don't know, their savior. That's what they think, anyway."

"Savior?"

"Maybe I am," said Daniel, and with such conviction. "Look where we are now." He raised his hands to the examples of wealth that lined his walls. "I suggested things as they came to mind, no matter how absurd. And they worked. They worked because my life had transformed into what was supposed to be fantasy.

"Do you even know what we do?" said Daniel. "To make a living, I mean. We sell organs to hospitals along the west coast. Hearts and livers and kidneys from the people we've eaten. Homeless and runaways, mostly. We put their bodies to good use. Does that sound like anything remotely possible, given the extent of our old lives?"

It seemed far-fetched within the bounds of my new understanding. But none of what he'd said addressed the fact that he'd gone four years without letting me know that he was alive.

"I know you think that I forgot about you," said Daniel, as if he'd read my mind. "The truth is that maybe I did."

Something sank inside my chest.

"I meant to bring you with me," said Daniel. "But I wanted it to be perfect for you. Beautiful. Not just some dirty shack in the woods. You deserved more than that."

"What?" I said.

"Our whole concept of vampires was larger than life. Romantic. We never imagined living like animals, scared for our fucking lives."

"If you could survive it," I said, "what makes you think I couldn't?"

"I'm trying to tell you it wasn't easy," said Daniel.

I felt worse than before. Insulted. It was as if he thought I was a child that needed protection from the life he'd made for himself.

"Imagine," said Daniel, in his defense, "if you came across a diamond, trapped beneath rock and coal. You could see a piece of it, so you knew for sure that it was there. And you knew it would be the perfect gift for someone. Someone very important to you. You wouldn't bring that person out to the pile of rock and say, 'Look what I've found for you!' You'd work away at all the shit surrounding the diamond. And once you'd held it in your hands, you'd have it cut and wrapped in a lavish box, and then present it as a real gift. Wouldn't you?"

Daniel's metaphor sounded crass. I wanted something tangible – something terrible that kept him away no matter how hard he tried to get back to me. Death, imprisonment, or even severe amnesia. Something more tragic than a gradual disinterest.

"I became so lost in the process of chipping away at that rock," said Daniel. "I must have forgotten why I'd started. Even when I'd removed the diamond, I..."

"Stop," I said.

"I have," said Daniel. "That's why I didn't hesitate when I saw you outside my apartment. What was it? Fifteen minutes before I had my teeth in your neck?"

"I meant shut the fuck up."

Daniel seemed taken aback. But he did as I said.

"Forget who we were for a minute. In the past. To each other." I paused. Because I wasn't sure that I could follow my own advice. "I don't know you anymore. And you sure as fuck don't know what I want in my life. Not now."

"David, we don't change all that much," he said.

"I said stop. You owe it to me. To shut the fuck up and listen for a minute."

Daniel began to smile, as if he found my outburst funny. "What do I owe you? You're in my home, wearing my clothes. I might have even saved your life. I know that Ian wanted you dead."

I pushed back the guilt he'd tried to force on me. "I'm not a fucking house guest. So don't sit there so smug!"

Daniel grabbed my face taut between his hands. He pushed his face against mine; bit my lip and shoved his tongue inside my mouth. It was like he thought I couldn't resist. That I would be enamored by his touch, and fall back in lust with him.

I sunk my teeth into the spongy tissue that reached for my throat. Daniel's blood rushed into my mouth, and he pulled away. I shoved him further, and he fell on to his back. Then I was on top of him with my hands around his neck. I pressed my weight against his torso and held him down.

I'll kill you as many times as it takes.

Daniel broke one of my hands from its grip. I balled it into a fist and struck him in the face.

I saw the juice flow from his nose, and found my hunger, and lashed out for the red with my tongue. His blood filled my stomach. Then I felt a sting at the base of my chin. Daniel had latched on to me with his fangs.

My grip on him loosened as we devoured each other. His legs wrapped around my waist, and he pulled me close, like when we were young. He guided my body so that our eyes met. With little acknowledgement, we ate at each other's mouths like we'd never been apart.

My cock grew stiff beneath my jeans. Daniel ripped it free in seconds. I wrestled him on to his chest, and pulled on his hips so that his ass stuck in the air. His pants came off. I smeared his ass with blood; spit on my cock and shoved it inside him.

After several thrusts, I fell on to Daniel and tried to suffocate him with my hands. "I'll kill you as many times as it takes."

"Do it," he said, with my fingers in his mouth. "I want to

fucking feel it this time."

I continued to fuck him, and watched for his eyes to roll back in his head. There was no hint of revenge or self-defense. I continued because it felt good.

Daniel turned over to face me, and pulled my hands back to his throat. He stopped breathing minutes later.

I shot myself inside him and fell asleep; waited for morning, for his return, for the answer to my question: Were we still in love?

FEELING WEEPY

"WHERE IS HE?" ASKED MY MOTHER, FIRST AT MY door, and then inside my bedroom. "The mom-across-the-street has been waiting all morning for you two to wake up. Says Daniel has a doctor's appointment."

"Not here," I said, still half asleep. "Obviously."

My mother opened my closet and looked inside, as if Daniel might have been hiding there. "Where is he? I need that woman out of my hair."

"Daniel doesn't spend the night," I said, as a reminder. "It freaks you guys out."

"I was once your age too, and told my parents what they wanted to hear," said my mother. "But really, David, do you know where he is?"

Daniel's mother came to our door soon after, in a panic. She said that many of his clothes were missing, that my father's lightweight suitcase was gone, and that his toiletries had disappeared from their place in the bathroom. Because of my relationship to Daniel, all fingers were pointed at me.

"Don't play with me," said his mother. "If you two were planning a little runaway trip together, it's time to fess up."

"If he's made any plans, I've been left out of them," I said, in honesty. At the time, I didn't see any cause for concern. True, I hadn't known Daniel to take part in the kind of pranks the missing items had suggested. But I knew that Daniel wouldn't take off for any real length of time without telling me. "You probably just pissed him off."

Unable to get answers from me, Daniel's mother called the police. They wouldn't file a missing person's report until he was gone for at least 48 hours. So we spent the next two days waiting. Our parents waited at home. I waited at school, and then at Jesse's house. If Daniel didn't come home, I thought he might at least make it to band practice.

"Is he going to be at the show on Friday?" asked Henry.

"I don't know," I said. "I don't know where he is. I don't know where he's going. And I don't know when he's coming back. I don't know fucking anything, because he didn't tell me he was leaving in the first place."

"Maybe he hinted at it," said Henry. "Like, if he was trying to be obscure? Maybe through some new lyrics. Doesn't he read you that shit, like it's poetry?"

"You want me to remember everything he said to me over the past, I don't know how many days? Then decide which time he meant to say, 'I'm taking off for a while. Just wanted to tell you through cryptic poetry, or interpretive dance.'"

Henry took on a look, like he hated me. "Im trying to help," he said. "If we're not going to play the show, I could make other plans."

"Then cancel it," I said.

We did. We canceled all of our shows.

When Daniel became an official missing person, I still didn't think he was gone for good. I only started to wish that we were rich. Because it was a time before cell phones were as common as shoes. If our families had a bit more money, we could have been a part of the elite group of high school students who communicated through such devices. I would have filled Daniel's voicemail with messages about how much of a cunt he was for making me talk to thirty people a day, for making me answer the same questions over and over again, and for having me tell the police that I didn't know a thing. I would tell him that I was sick of jerking off, and that closeted theater students weren't exactly substitutes for his beautiful fucking mouth. Later, I'd apologize. I'd text him, asking if I'd done something wrong. Whatever it was, I would tell him that I'd make it up to him. But we didn't have cell phones. We had no way of communicating at all. Everything I meant to say to Daniel was whispered into my pillow at night or screamed inside my head while I cried on the bathroom floor.

His parents were in hysterics. His mother believed that he'd been murdered by a cult inspired by the *satanic* music we listened to. His father thought he'd overdosed on drugs under a bridge. I just knew that he was gone.

So I mourned my friend, my brother, my first true love. Because I'd never said, "I love you," it made it all the worse. Sixteen years old, and the only person I truly cared about was gone. It was like part of me had been cut off. But there was no preordained rehabilitation for the loss of ten years of comfort and sanity.

I fell into the usual teenage coping mechanisms. My arms became a cutting board for razor blades and broken pieces of glass. I took pills to fall asleep at night and smoked whatever I could get my hands on. When my grades dropped, I was forced into school counseling. When that didn't work, I convinced my parents to let me take the proficiency exam and drop out of high school early. The compromise was that I enroll in the local community college and get some sort of degree.

After the initial pain subsided, there were still nights I'd wake up covered in sweat. I'd see Daniel in front of me, suffering the fate of whatever my imagination had cooked up for him. Each time I thought I'd moved on, I was reminded of my friend through the visions of his death. He stayed with me in the most bittersweet of ways. Through my fondest memories and the manifestations of my fears.

BREAKFAST OF CHAMPIONS

MY EYELIDS WAVERED IN A HALF-OPEN STATE. THE images before me were barely in focus: blood-stained marble and a web of drool, spun from my lip.

It didn't bother me to find myself naked on the floor of Daniel's apartment. It didn't even bother me to find him missing from my side, despite the fact that I'd watched him die the night before. Because I could hear footsteps under a symphonic melody that turned to crushing blast-beats and overdriven guitar. It was proof that Daniel was alive and roaming his apartment. And that he was exercising the same musical taste we had in high school.

I stumbled towards the kitchen and found Daniel perched over the stovetop. He wore a Darkthrone shirt and a pair of pajama bottoms, and poured a crimson syrup over eggs. Several days before, I would have had to guess at the ingredients of such a concoction. But it became safe to assume that he ate blood with everything.

Daniel looked up, smiled, and turned off the MP3 player that was built into the wall. "Sleep well?" he asked.

I nodded and examined his face. There was evidence of broken blood vessels in the yellow bruising that surrounded his nose and cheeks. Other than that, he looked healed. No signs of strangulation. No fractured bones.

"I hope you still like eggs," said Daniel. "I've added something extra to accommodate your new taste."

I looked at the frying pan and smelled the morning's meal.

"Maybe you should get cleaned up first," said Daniel. "I'll get you a towel." He scooped some eggs on to a plate and disappeared into another room.

I sampled the breakfast in his absence. It was strangely delicious. The blood worked almost like a seasoning. In its fried, coagulated state, it provided a textural crunch. I tried to imagine whether I'd have liked such a thing before my transformation. But Daniel interrupted me, and shoved a towel in my face.

"You remember where the bathroom is," said Daniel, with a smirk.

I nodded and took the towel from him. "Thanks."

***

I saw my face in the bathroom mirror. It was a mess of dried blood and flakes, and other crusted fluids.

I showered, and rinsed off the once-arousing filth.

What next? Where do I even begin to go from here?

My thoughts disappeared under the water. I bathed in oblivion.

***

Daniel sat alone at a small, glass table. He looked up as I approached, and motioned to a plate full of the remaining breakfast that he'd prepared.

I sat down next to him. Daniel watched as I ate in silence. Eventually, I couldn't stand it. "What happens now? What am I supposed to do?"

"What do you mean?" he said, and sipped from a glass of mineral water.

"I've been working towards things, you know. Been trying to make a life for myself. To say this is an inconvenience... It's about the nicest way I can put it."

"You want to go back to school?" said Daniel. "Get your degree? What are you studying anyway?"

"Film," I said.

"Why film?"

"I don't know," I said. "To communicate something. Tell a story. Whatever. What the fuck do you care?"

Daniel put down his glass and folded his hands in front of him. "Why tell a story? What good is that?"

"What?" I said, nearly shouting at him. "What the fuck good is anything?"

Daniel stayed calm, which felt even more condescending. "I'm trying to help. You asked me, a moment ago, what you're supposed to do. You obviously don't find this new identity to be so inherently wonderful."

"I murdered someone," I said.

"I heard," said Daniel, as if the act was something ordinary. "You say you like stories? I have a story that could change your life."

"You don't think it's changed enough already?"

"Maybe," said Daniel. "But it's a story you'd hear sooner or later. At least, if you decide to spend your time with others like us."

"Okay."

"But hearing this story is not my only proposal."

"I'm lost," I said.

"I think that we should act on it." Daniel leaned towards me, as if he was going to crawl up on the table and grab hold of my skin. "Aren't you curious?" he asked. "About the origin of the vampire?"

"I'm sure you're going to tell me," I said, even though I barely cared.

"No," said Daniel. "Astrid will do it."

"That bitch who tied me up?"

"She knows it better than I do," said Daniel. "Get dressed.

I'll bring you to her."

"What about...?" I meant to say, "Us," as in the two of us who'd fucked the night before at the foot of Daniel's bed; the undiscussed us that no history lesson could put to rest. But Daniel made it clear that we had no time to linger. He excused himself without another word, and left me alone, still half-naked in a bath towel.

ACADEMIA AND I

"HAVE YOU DECIDED ON A MAJOR?" ASKED MY community college counselor.

I shook my head, "No."

"Have you at least given it some thought?"

"Maybe music?" I said. It was the only subject I'd showed interest in. At least, that could translate into an academic discipline. But really, I hadn't glanced at a sheet of music during all my years of playing guitar.

At my counselor's advice, I signed up for an introductory course in music theory. Within a few weeks, I came to hate the process of intellectualizing pitch and melody. I'd learned to play my instrument through simple instruction, then by emulating metal records, and finally, by writing my own songs. Sitting in class, learning scales on a piano, didn't seem very punk rock to me. What was I going to do with a music degree anyway? Play in an orchestra?

I found myself back in the counselor's office, listening to the same question: "Have you decided on a major?"

"Not music," I said.

"What are you interested in?" she asked.

"Music. Which is why I don't want to study it." I didn't care to explain myself. So she kept probing in resignation to the tasks required of her.

"Do you have any other interests?" she asked. "Or are you not interested in taking an..." Her eyes darted back and forth, as if she should have a thesaurus nailed to the wall. "Interest in your education?"

"I have parents," I said. "They want me to go to a university. And I guess I'd always imagined myself going off to study somewhere." Except I'd never thought about what would happen past college. Or about what school I'd want to attend. I just knew it wasn't the local community college.

***

One night, while surfing the web for California universities and their lists of majors, I put on a copy of Jörg Buttgereit's *Nekromantik*, a German cult film from the late 1980's. A friend had loaned me a bootlegged DVD of the film. He said it was full of the "disgusting shit" I was into, probably because he'd seen a few album covers for some of the death metal bands I listened to.

The film did capture my attention. Maybe it was the catchy, synth-based soundtrack, the DIY aesthetic, or the fact that the film's ending (a man stabs himself in the stomach to induce orgasm) caused me both to laugh and contemplate what a beautiful thing I'd witnessed. I couldn't help but feel that it was a sign. The film ended, and I turned back to my computer screen. The cursor hovered over a link on the University of California, Santa Cruz, website. The text read, *Film and Digital Media.*

The *Nekromantik* film had reeked of a small budget. I didn't know how much Jörg Buttgereit had spent to produce his movie, but I felt confident that I could make something similar, if only I knew how.

Right then and there, I decided to study film.

I hadn't already learned to make movies on my own, like I

had with music. The academic process would be the only one I knew until I finished school. I needed the technical knowledge. Because I didn't know anything about cameras, lights, or whatever else was involved.

But making movies was something to get excited about. My band had fallen apart, and I'd become a social recluse. The fact that I'd felt something while watching Buttgereit's film was as significant of an event as any I could think of. And I wanted that power: to reach out to a stranger and make him feel.

I set my plan in motion, and told my parents and some of my friends. Just as soon, they began to ask what I wanted to make my movies about. No one had ever questioned why I spent hours practicing metal riffs on my guitar. But whenever I mentioned filmmaking, I was met with the assumption that I should have something to say.

So I came up with my message pretty quickly: "Fuck you." Abrasive art had become second nature to me. If I was going to sit in a classroom to learn my craft, I thought I'd better have some fun with it. The mark of my personal success became how many of my peers took offense. I started with brutal depictions of violence – all poorly executed – and moved on to sexual assault. If a classmate expressed an issue with my piece, I'd write his character into the next project and film his cinematic violation and murder.

But it soon became a bore. I realized that I didn't have anything to say, and that it bothered me. Something about college had turned everyone around me into *thoughtful* artists, each with their own philosophy on how to change the world. I just came up with ways to murder people. My films came off as embarrassing compared to the works of my peers, self-proclaimed intellectual philanthropists.

I looked back on my decision to study film and the piece of cinema that had inspired me. The corpse in *Nekromantik* assumed new meaning. I hadn't experienced a satisfying relationship since Daniel. Even my sex with Peter and his friends lacked real physical gratification. It was as if Daniel was my corpse, the decaying beast from my past. He kept me from moving on, from relating to other people. In *Nekromantik*, the protagonist had to kill in order to get himself off. Even then, he didn't find real pleasure until he destroyed himself. I had to kill Daniel in my mind. It seemed like film might be a way for me to exorcise him from my thoughts.

So I produced a short, like a ritual, in which I performed – what I thought would be – my last student film death. Peter played Daniel. We pretended to fuck and then commit suicide together. It was like a poor-man's *Romeo and Juliet*, without the family strife.

I shared the film with my class, and no one had much to say. But it seemed like I might have accomplished what I'd set out for. By the time I transferred to the University of California, Santa Cruz, my nightmares of Daniel had disappeared. I told myself that I would look for inspiration in new places, and take on subjects for my films that would bring people together.

THE MYTH IS ALIVE

IN THE STREET, OUTSIDE DANIEL'S APARTMENT, I asked where we were going.

"To Astrid's," said Daniel.

I'd assumed that Astrid lived below him, perhaps in the interrogation room. But I learned that vampires had come to live in their own homes, flats, apartments, and houses. They'd moved up in the world since the time of Oregonian barns.

We traveled by foot, bus, and subway. I watched the street names as we passed by, and looked for landmarks that I'd remember. I wanted to make sure that I could find my out. Just in case things got out of hand and I needed to escape. But when we arrived, I found that I was already familiar with the neighborhood. Astrid lived in the Sunset District, not five blocks from Mika's apartment.

"To what do I owe the visit?" asked Astrid.

"I want him to know about us," said Daniel. "About our history."

Astrid stood quietly for a moment, and looked me over. Then she invited us inside.

The interior of her home was modest. At least compared to Daniel's. She told us to sit on her couch, which looked like something from a second-hand store, while she made some tea.

"What have you figured out?" said Astrid, once she'd offered me a mug and a small vial of blood to go along with it. "On your own?"

"I'm not sure," I said.

"You know that you're a vampire," she said. "What does that mean to you?"

I didn't think that I'd be the one answering questions. But I tried to play along. For as long as I could. "There's the obvious part. We drink blood."

"Have you been able to control your desire?" said Astrid. "For blood."

"I'm pretty sure," I said. "But the first time I..."

"I know," said Astrid. "It's a powerful urge. But one that becomes easier to get a hold of. I promise. What else have you learned?"

I looked at Daniel through the corner of my eye. "When we die, it doesn't last very long. So can we? Die, I mean."

Astrid smiled, like what I'd said was childish. "Many wounds will bring us death, in the human sense of the word. Though, yes, we do often come back to life. We regenerate cells at a faster rate than most. But there are rumors that you may have heard from old books and movies. For example, that a vampire will die for good if pierced through the heart. That one's true. I'll explain why in a moment. But first, is there anything else you've learned on your own?"

It was early in the day, and light poured in from the windows. I thought of the films I'd seen about vampires, and the band I listened to that would only show themselves at night. "Sunlight doesn't seem to be a problem."

"Luckily," said Astrid, "that bit is storybook nonsense. If anything, it's a metaphor."

"A metaphor for what?" I asked.

"We are born of a certain darkness," said Astrid, and she sounded almost pained. "At least, in the eyes of God."

"Excuse me?" I said, as if I'd heard incorrectly. I turned to Daniel, but he averted his eyes.

"This is what I brought you to hear," said Daniel.

"You don't believe in God," I said.

"Would you excuse us for a moment?" said Daniel to Astrid. He took me by the hand and pulled me from my seat – to the kitchen, where we were alone enough to whisper and not be heard.

"I told you it was a story," said Daniel. "If it's true or not... Who cares?"

"Who cares?"

"Every society, every culture, has a story. Something that binds them together. God is not the hero in our story. But He still plays an important role."

"I'm twenty-years-old," I said. "I don't need to sit through another Sunday school lesson."

"Astrid believes that God is real," said Daniel. "And that He may affect us in a real way."

"Good for her," I said. "But I don't believe in God, and neither do you. Unless you've decided to become a fucking sheep. God is just a way for people to manipulate each other. You used to understand that."

"Do you believe in vampires?" said Daniel. "They're just made up, right? A way for people to scare each other? Like God?"

"Fuck you."

"What reason does she have to lie?" said Daniel.

"I don't know," I said. "She might even believe what she's saying. Doesn't make it true."

"Would it hurt to listen?"

"Daniel, there's enough shit for me to worry about right now. I don't have time for this."

"You told me that you like to make movies," said Daniel. "Right? That you want to tell your own stories. Why would you be interested in something like that unless you cared that people were listening?"

"What's your point?"

"I have a theory," said Daniel. "That you've been hurt. By me. By others, I'm sure. That you've lost hope in most of us. But it doesn't mean you've stopped trying. You want to feel like somebody cares; like your life will have meant something at the end of it all."

"I have a theory that you're a selfish asshole," I said. "You want to talk about stories? How about ours? Let's talk about what happened last night."

"No," said Daniel. "Right now, I'd rather help you along in your new life. If that's a selfish thing to want, then yes, I'm selfish."

I was getting nowhere with Daniel, so I stopped trying. I crossed my arms and let him speak at me. Did my best to stop listening. But he was so earnest, so good at pushing himself into my head.

"You can believe what you want," said Daniel. "The difference between Astrid's story and what we used to read about on album covers is that we can change the course of hers. Listen to what she has to say. Help me do what needs to be done. People won't just pay attention to you or watch your fucking movies. They'll follow you."

***

Daniel managed to wrangle me back on to the couch. He convinced Astrid to continue where she left off.

"We don't have a sacred text," said Astrid. "No Bible or anything like that. Our story has been passed down by word of mouth. When you've been alive as long as I have, you develop a discernment. An ability to know the truth when you hear it. The man who told me this story; he had that ability too.

"He said that our origin went back around 2,000 years, to the time of Jesus of Nazareth. You've heard of him? The one the Christians call the Son of God."

I rolled my eyes, and turned to Daniel. His face remained a solemn mask.

"He was, as far as I know," said Astrid. "Spirit made flesh."

"You think I've never heard of Jesus?" I said. "We live in the United States. This country was founded on Christianity. And no Christian I've ever met has said a word about vampires."

"Our story never made it into the gospels," said Astrid. "Because it suggests an unpopular notion."

"Yeah? What's that?"

"That God is fallible," said Astrid. "You've heard of the fast in the desert?" She recited scripture, as if the page were right in front of her. "'*Then Jesus was led by the Spirit into the wilderness to be tempted by the devil. After fasting forty days and forty nights, he was hungry. The tempter came to him and said, 'If you are the Son of God, tell these stones to become bread.'*

"Jesus answered, 'It is written: Man shall not live on bread alone, but on every word that comes from the mouth of God.'"

"Okay," I said, unimpressed by her ability to memorize such a popular book.

"It's written in the gospels that Jesus was tempted twice more in the desert," said Astrid. "But there's more to it than that. More than what was written."

"Of course," I said with all the sarcasm I could muster.

"Daniel tells me you're familiar," said Astrid. "That you might have heard the stories in church when you were young?"

"Uh huh."

"Think back to the story of creation. Of Heaven and Hell. You've heard of Lucifer, the morning star, who's name was changed to Satan? He was an angel. The most beautiful in Heaven. He came to believe that he was better than God. In fact, he started a war to prove it. Lucifer convinced a legion of angels to fight in his name."

"Yeah, I said I've heard the stories."

"So you know what happened," said Astrid. "Lucifer lost, and..."

"I know," I said. "He was banished to Hell. What does any of this have to do with us?"

"Lucifer fought against God and lost," said Astrid. "Then for the first time in a millenia, he had the chance to face his foe again. In such a vulnerable state. Out there in the wilderness. God made into man.

"Lucifer had a goal stronger than temptation. He wanted to dethrone God."

"Daniel," I said, as if I could ignore Astrid. "Can we please go?"

Daniel wouldn't look at me. He unbuckled his belt and pulled it from the loops in his jeans; held it taught in his hands. It was a strange gesture. Did he mean to threaten me? I began to laugh, until he was behind me, with the belt across my throat.

"Listen," said Daniel, fierce into my ear. "Please."

I tried to escape his grip, but he'd become strong in our time apart. There was no budging from my place on the couch.

"Go on," said Daniel to Astrid.

Astrid seemed taken aback. Though, after a moment, she continued. "Our story says that during one of the nights in the desert, Lucifer asked Jesus, the God-man, why only He could come to earth in such a form. If humankind were to have free will, there should be another choice – another messiah to follow. Not the prophets of other religions, because they spoke of things too similar. Lucifer wanted a piece of himself made into man.

"In his emaciated state, Jesus let something slip. He suggested that human form was not granted to God, alone.

"It was as if Lucifer had been given permission. Before he'd heard Jesus' words, he'd never thought to try. But he wouldn't waste time. Wouldn't find a virgin bride and wait for her child to grow old. Instead, he'd fuse his nature with man's heart, the gateway to the soul, and flow through his veins. Lucifer's touch would be in every drop of blood."

Daniel let up, and allowed for me to breath. I coughed, and reached behind me, because I thought the story was over. But as I tried to pry him off, Daniel tightened his grip again.

"We are Lucifer's children," said Astrid. "No act or prayer can save our souls from Hell.

"Our father gave us a thirst for blood. So that we might spread his seed. One fallen angel could never overthrow Heaven. But a legion of vampires might march on St. Peter's gate. That is our purpose."

Again, I was allowed to breath. But the story continued on.

"God was not a fool," said Astrid. "He knew of Jesus' weakness as a man. His mistake in the desert. So God brought forth His followers to hunt us down. They've stalked us for 2,000 years. Slaughtered us in the Crusades, and after. There are few vampires now. Most, who survived, live in solitude.

"I've lived most of my life alone. Sometimes among others.

We've never been more than three or four together. Not until Daniel found us and brought us back into the world. He showed us that people no longer believe in God the way they used to. And that vampires have become a myth for your entertainment. For your books and films and television.

"It took Daniel some time to convince us that we don't have to live in fear. Because there's no one left to believe in us. No one to hunt us down.

"Until you nearly killed Daniel. Pierced him through the chest, and so near to his heart – the gateway to his soul. We had to be sure you weren't one of God's servants. Daniel's assured us that you were just afraid. That it was an accident. I've come to trust him when he tells me..." She hesitated, and looked me over, bound by Daniel's belt. "That you're a friend."

I sat, stunned, and retraced her words in my head, as if they might become less absurd. Astrid had delivered the most outrageous story I'd ever heard. And with such sincerity.

"Ian and I, and several others," said Astrid, "believe that Daniel is the one to fulfill our purpose. We believe he will raise the army necessary to wage our war on Heaven. Without that army, we're damned."

"You're wrong," said Daniel.

Astrid's composure fell apart at what he'd said. "What?"

"You will have your army," said Daniel. "But I won't be the one to lead it."

"Then who?" said Astrid.

Daniel removed the belt from around my neck and placed his hand upon my head, like a crown.

***

I slammed the door behind me, and barreled down the steps outside of Astrid's house.

There was only so much I could deal with. My limit had been up for several days. It seemed like the only way to get back to reality was to escape to somewhere familiar. The closest place I knew of was Mika's apartment, nearby.

But my exodus was too slow. I could already hear Daniel, running up behind me.

"Wait," he said, and rushed in front of me to block my way. "Just hear me out."

"I've been listening," I said. "Done a whole lot of it, actually. I'm done."

"Forget all that stuff about God," he said as I tried to push past him. "Think about the rest. You and me, raising an army to do whatever we want?"

"Why the fuck would anyone listen to you?" I said.

"If they won't listen to me, they'll listen to you. Or maybe the both of us," said Daniel, power-walking beside me. "I'm going back to Grass Valley in a couple of days. I want you to come with me."

Our hometown? Why would he want to go back there?

"I don't care."

"It could be like starting over," said Daniel. "We'll go back to school..."

"I'm already in school," I reminded him.

"I don't mean as students," he said. "We'll go to our middle-school. Maybe elementary."

It occurred to me what he was suggesting. "Are you telling me that you want to bite kids? Turn kids into vampires? You're a piece of shit."

"They still have imagination," said Daniel. "When you're

young, you think you can do anything. Be anything." He began to fall behind me. "I'm leaving tomorrow. If you change your mind, you know where to find me."

REPLACEMENT

I REMEMBERED CALLING MIKA FOR THE FIRST time after our trip to Napa, and asking if I could spend the night at her apartment in San Francisco. So that I could save an hour's drive to work. I remembered not sleeping, because Mika had just broken up with her girlfriend and I was the most convenient form of therapy. I stayed awake with her, and without a grudge. It was strange to hear her share so much of her life, love, pain, and happiness. Because we'd only known each other for a short time.

When Daniel left, I never divulged my feelings to anyone. Sure, I mentioned a few details to school counselors. But never more than what was obvious.

My first night in Mika's apartment, I listened to her talk for hours. She curled up next to me on her bed and cried. In a way, I didn't want the night to end. I felt useful for once. Mika trust me with her secrets, and I felt a responsibility to keep them safe.

"Any time you need a place to stay in the city," said Mika, the next day in a voicemail, "you have a spot reserved on my bed."

I took her up on the offer most every time I booked a job with Fetisynth. If my shoot was on a Friday, I'd spend an extra day with her on the weekend. We'd go to art shows in the Mission and watch splatter films at the Castro Theater. At night, we'd climb to the rooftops of nightclubs and throw candy at fucked-up patrons.

Mika became like my best friend, though she rarely took part in the life I had away from her. And I rarely interfered with her life apart from me.

When I got kicked out of my dorm room for winter break, I called Mika, and asked if I could stay for more than a couple of nights. She said, "Yes," but with a caveat. I needed to help her move.

Mika's neighborhood wasn't under rent control. The price of her apartment was driving her into debt. She had to downsize, and move across town with a few roommates.

She'd done me enough favors in the past, so of course, I agreed to help. I also extended the offer for her to spend Christmas with my family. I'd meant it as an act of reciprocation for all she'd done – to give her a few days off and some home-cooked meals.

But on Christmas morning, as we sat together on my mother's couch, I realized that I'd made a mistake. Both my mother and Mr. Brion, and my father and Mrs. Nevenhart, had decided to spend Christmas together. Supposedly, on my behalf. But neither couple had attempted to patch up the emotional havoc they'd wreaked on each other's lives.

My father immediately began to criticize my mother for her home décor. He said it made her look like poor and like peasant. My mother told him, in so many words, that he'd grown ugly with age, and that she, at least, still had a real man.

Mrs. Nevenhart had had a few drinks by the time we got to opening presents. She told everyone to stop what they were doing and wait while she ran across the street. She returned with a stocking full of Daniel's old belongings – artifacts she'd kept in memory of her dead son.

"This is Daniel," said Mrs. Nevenhart, as she held up a polaroid in front of Mika's face. "Look at his eyes. Who couldn't love those eyes?"

"Darling," said my father, but he followed it with nothing.

"He's my son," said Mrs. Nevenhart. "It's important that we remember him."

"We do," said my mother. She encouraged the rest of us to nod. Even Mika rocked her head in agreement.

But we couldn't stop Mrs. Nevenhart from crying. We couldn't prevent her from tilting her glass; from spilling brandy across the polaroid.

"Look what I've done." Mrs. Nevenhart gasped. "A napkin! Someone get a napkin. Please!"

No one had a chance to react before Mrs. Nevenhart moved on to her next request. "David, don't you think you should make a speech on behalf of your brother? Or what would you call him? You slut."

My father pounced in front of Mrs. Nevenhart, and wrapped his palm around her mouth. "Sorry, I'm so sorry," she said, muffled beneath his fingers as he dragged her from the room.

***

That night, when I was alone with Mika, I apologized.

"Why do you think I don't visit my family for the holidays?" she said. "It's not because they're dead. Everyone's parents are fucked up. I get it. All the more reason to let you crash at my place."

The damage was done, and Mika hadn't run for the hills. We drove back to San Francisco, and carried on like usual. I believed I had a true friend. One who'd stand by me through anything.

THE DOOR UNLOCKS IN MY OWN SAFE HAVEN

I TRIED THE DOORBELL FIRST AND THEN knocked. Several seconds went by, and I tried each one again.

"Mika!" I shouted. "I know you're in there!" It was a lie. She could have been anywhere. But I didn't have my cell phone on me. If Mika wasn't home, my only hope was to draw out one of her roommates. Maybe they'd give me a clue as to her whereabouts.

After several minutes, I gave up. I walked a few blocks further until I came across a convenience store with a pay phone in the lot.

Somehow, I'd managed to keep my wallet on me. I searched the coin pouch, and found two quarters; put them in the phone and dialed Mika's number.

"Hello?" Her voice sounded far away, and like a cheap imitation.

"Mika, hey," I said. "I stopped by your place. Are you at work, or something?"

"No."

"Oh. Where are you?"

"At my friend, Angela's," said Mika. "I've been staying here since... You know."

I'd been so preoccupied with Daniel, my transformation, and all the rest. I hadn't even thought about what Mika had been going through. "So, um, how are you?"

"I don't know," said Mika. Her voice trailed off into dead air, then came back. "The same, I guess."

"Do you think I could stop by?"

"I'd have to ask Angela."

I didn't want to rush her, but I needed an answer. "Is she there? I kind of need to talk to you."

"You want to give me a hint?" said Mika.

"What do you mean?"

She sounded on the verge of exhaustion. "I'm a little fragile. A little less open to all topics of conversation."

I almost hung up. To allow her to mourn in peace. But I considered my relationship to Mika, and stacked it up against the probable lack of interest she had in her roommate's old life.

To ease my guilt, I fed her a white lie. "It's not that big of a deal," I said. "It would just be cool to see you."

"Yeah, I guess it would be good to see you too," said Mika.

"You guess?" I said, and meant to play with her.

"Fine," said Mika. "Come over." There was a muffled sound on the line. Then, "Angela says it's okay. I'll text you her address."

"I'm on a payphone," I said.

"What? Why?"

"It's a long story."

"So do you have something to write down her address with?"

***

A young woman opened the door. "You must be David," she

said.

I nodded. "Angela?"

She held the door for me, and said, "Come in. Mika's in the living room."

I followed Angela through the foyer, past a small kitchenette, and into a cluttered room with a coffee table, television, and a long, green couch on which Mika had curled up with a blanket and bowl of cereal.

Mika scooped her body upwards and slid her legs over the edge of the couch. So that I'd have room to sit.

"What are you watching?" I asked.

She set her bowl on the table and exchanged it for a remote control. "Something forgettable." The volume on the TV dropped at her press of a button. Mika hugged me. "Thanks for stopping by. I know I was a grouch on the phone, but it is good to see you."

"You look good," I said, even though her skin was chalky pale and her eyes bloodshot.

"Don't lie," she said. "It's not going to make me feel better."

"Well, considering..."

Mika took a bite from her bowl of Corn Flakes. "What are you doing in the city today? Don't you have school?"

"I'm allowed a day off every once in a while," I said.

She ran a hand across her body, as if to display her wardrobe – a dirty shirt and sweat pants. I think she'd meant to say that she agreed.

"I ran into an old friend," I said, and considered my next words. "You know the guy I grew up with? Daniel?"

Her face appeared to change, as if a flood of pain had washed her over. I realized that I hadn't only mentioned the name of my friend. Her dead roommate was also named Daniel.

Mika tried to play it off, like she hadn't been affected. "I remember you talking about him. He went missing when you were young, right?"

"Yeah."

"That's who you ran into?"

I nodded.

"David, that's a really big deal," said Mika. "You were, like, in love with him."

"Yeah," I said, frankly.

"So what happened?" she asked.

How do I tell her?

You could start with something she might believe?

And what do you think that would be?

My mind raced through the events of the past few days; past everything that had to do with vampires. I landed on something that could be interpreted as rational.

"He wants me to go back home with him," I said. "To Grass Valley."

"To see your parents?" said Mika. "Don't they think he's dead?"

"I guess so."

I saw a kind of energy in Mika. Something like anticipation. It was the opposite of a metaphorical dying, as in dying to hear my story. She'd emerged with new life, ready to put her thoughts towards something other than her sadness.

"David?" said Mika.

I wanted to go on – to keep her focused on what I'd said. But I'd caught sight of the television, and the evidence of my violence.

The news was on and muted. I saw footage of myself, huddled in a small dormitory, ripping open a fellow student, and being wrestled to the ground. My face was shown, splattered with blood and with a detached kind of expression.

Louis must have turned over his footage to a local television station.

Why don't you say something? Make Mika see what you are.

Because I care about her. More than Daniel, and so more than anyone in the world.

Then why would you have her think of you as something other than a murderer? You're the reason she's a wreck, hiding on her friend's couch.

Because it would ruin her, and...

And what?

Because I didn't mean to kill "her" Daniel. I have a disease, or something. My blood is sick. None of this is my fault.

I flung myself towards Mika, almost like an instinct. I wanted to cover her. To keep her from seeing the screen.

She jumped from the couch and held tight to her blanket, as if it were a barrier between us that could keep me from getting closer. "David, what the fuck is wrong with you?"

"Did you see the TV?" I asked.

Mika looked towards the screen. "What's on the TV?"

I turned my head and saw a flow of images. None of them had to do with me. The news had given way to a commercial break. I blew the air from my lungs, and leaned back in relief.

"David, what's going on?"

Mika's friend, Angela, came into the room. "Is everything okay?"

"Yes," I said, and nearly laughed. I couldn't help it. It was like a nervous tick I'd just developed. "Everything's perfect."

The girls exchanged signals with their hands, as if to decipher what mania had taken me over.

"I think you'd better go," said Angela. She pulled me from the couch and pushed at my back; prodded me along towards the front door.

Near the kitchenette, I spun to face the both of them. "Wait," I said. "But I know..." The secret I'd held back became a poison in my stomach. It boiled in me and rose up, and fought its way to the top of my throat.

I watched, as if in slow motion, while Mika fell apart. My tears flowed the same as hers. A purge. My catharsis.

"I know who killed Daniel," I said.

Mika and I bawled together.

FRIENDLY FIRE

THE UNIVERSITY OF CALIFORNIA, SANTA CRUZ, was built above the city, in the mountains, on 2,000 acres of land. A meadow of wild grass sprawled out behind the dormitory that housed me. The grass stopped at the edge of a small forest.

I used to look at the woods from my dorm-room window, and think of ideas for student films that I might shoot there. One day, I entered the forest in search of a location for one of my shorts.

There was a familiar smell that caught my attention as I stepped beyond the trees. I followed the scent, and saw a cloud of smoke rise from behind a head of matted, brown dreadlocks.

"Hey!" I shouted, friendly-like, and raised my hand to wave.

No one answered. The boy with the dreadlocks only rocked his body, as if to a silent beat, and puffed from a small, glass pipe.

I'd meant to introduce myself, and ask the boy what he knew about the area. As I approached, I saw that he wore a pair of ear buds. I understood why he hadn't responded to my call.

I stepped in front of the boy, and saw that he held a lit match. We met eyes and he jumped back, startled. His grip on the match faltered. It fell into the brush. A patch of dried leaves lit up in a cyclone of smoke and cinder.

I responded in a way that was neither heroic nor an illustration of common sense. If I had the ability to do it over again, I would have taken off my shirt and attempted to smother the flames.

But I ran as fast as I could in the opposite direction. Squirrels and other wildlife ran beside me. So did the stoned hippie. We all charged full-speed towards the dormitory.

The boy flipped his shit, and started screaming. For a time, his wails were louder than the fire engine sirens I heard in the distance.

His cries ultimately served my best interest. As I entered the mess hall and hid amongst the swarm of students, I saw the boy – through the window – accosted by campus police. He must have made enough of a scene to distract from the fact that two people had been seen running from the forest fire. Not just one.

I heard rumors throughout the following week. The boy had been convicted of arson and expelled from school. I never came forward to admit my role in what I thought had been an accident. Instead, I called Mika and shared my secret guilt.

"Do you think they would have gone easier on him?" I said. "If I'd explained what happened?"

"If they didn't believe him, why would they believe you?" said Mika. "Don't fuck up your education because you feel sorry for some granola motherfucker. I mean, you were planning for your student film. He was just getting high."

"Yeah, but he didn't mean to..."

"David." Mika interrupted me. "It's a school. A bureaucracy. Someone has to go down for the *crime*. It's either you, or him, or both of you together. Who was holding the match?"

"He was," I said, and tried to align myself with her rationalization.

"So what are you getting so worked up about?"

I told myself that Mika was right. The boy was guilty, and I was an innocent bystander.

But what if the situation had been reversed? What if I'd called Mika to tell her of my expulsion from the university? What if I'd said that a fellow student had scared me in the woods, and I'd accidentally lit the place on fire?

I hoped that Mika would stand by me, no matter what; that she'd take my side because of friendship, and not on the basis of her moral logic. Because a much greater crime had been committed, and I wasn't sure if it was my fault.

I bit into her roommate, much like the stoned Santa Cruzian had lit the match. But there had been an accomplice to my murder – Daniel, my blood, or perhaps the devil himself. If Mika couldn't see that I was a victim too, then I'd have no one left to turn to.

HAVE A LITTLE FAITH

ANGELA LAID INTO ME. "IF YOU HAVE ANY INFORmation about who killed her roommate..." She pointed her finger at Mika. "Now's the time to say so."

I tried to ease into the truth by delivering just a piece of it. "Daniel. My old friend. He's the one who killed him."

A croak festered up from my weeping friend. "Why?"

"Jesus," said Angela. "Do you know where he is?" Angela descended into her own world, and became preoccupied by whatever tasks she'd set out for herself. "Uh, the phone. I'll get the phone."

"David?" said Mika, and her eyes pleaded with me for answers.

I could refrain from telling the whole truth. But I couldn't flat-out lie to Mika. "He was trying to get to me," I said, even though it wasn't a direct answer to her question. Daniel turned me into a vampire – in some sense – to bring me back into his life. To get to me.

Angela reemerged from the kitchenette and pounded at her phone in a frenzied staccato.

"What are you doing?" I said.

"Calling the police," said Angela.

"No, don't do that," I said, and tried to grab her phone.

Angela pulled away from me. "What the fuck is wrong with you?"

"But..."

"Why don't you want me to call the police?" Angela turned to Mika. "This guy's your fucking friend? He's not acting a whole lot like it. Tell me you want him to leave, and I'll kick his ass to the curb."

"I don't know," said Mika, in a stutter.

The girls stared at me, as if to wait for my next action – the one that would define me as friend or foe.

What if I just tell the cops where Daniel lives?

But he didn't really kill Mika's roommate. Not literally.

They'd put him in jail, though, wouldn't they? He needs to be locked up.

How long could they hold him without evidence? And what would Daniel do if he escaped?

He'd come after me.

That's what you should tell the girls.

"You can't call the police," I said. "Because Daniel will come after me. At least, his friends will."

Angela finally appeared to take me seriously. She put down her phone. The animosity in her appeared to dry up.

"You don't know him," I said, and hoped that I sounded as scared as I felt. "Neither of you know him."

***

Angela shoved me in her bathroom and locked the door behind us. "I don't know who this Daniel guy is, or what's going on. But Mika's been through enough. She doesn't need any more of this shit. Tell me what's going on, or I kick you out and call the cops. Understand?"

"I do."

"So?" She pushed me on to the toilet and stared down. "You turn into a fucking mute?"

"Daniel killed Daniel. What else do you want me to say?"

"Why? What does this have to do with you? And why don't you want me to call the police?" She grabbed a pair of shears and held them out, like she might cut me.

"What are you going to do with those?" I asked.

"Just answer the questions," she said. I could see that her hands were shaking.

"Fine," I said. "You want the truth?" My mind began to purge, so that I wouldn't have to keep up with so many lies. I'd just hold on to the one that kept her from thinking I was a killer. "Daniel's a vampire. He bit Mika's roommate. Or ate him. Whatever."

"You think this is a fucking joke?" said Angela.

"I'm a vampire too."

"Stop it," she said, "Or..."

I stood and backed her against the wall. Angela lashed out with the shears. But I was no longer afraid of the harm she might inflict on me. After all, I'd heal in a couple of hours. "Or what?"

There was a knock at the door. "You guys?" said Mika. Her voice was weak. "What's going on?"

I snatched the shears from Angela and unlocked the bathroom door. As I stood between the two frightened girls, I considered what to do. I'd come to be with Mika so that I might find shelter in my former life. But that life was over. There were no more dreams of a brighter future. I was wanted for murder, and had been turned into a creature of legend. I didn't need help from Mika. But she might have needed it from me.

If Daniel and Astrid planned to turn the world upside down, Mika was in danger. Even more so because of her proximity to me. I needed to show her the truth, and protect her from harm. The only obstacle was her will to believe.

"You guys?" said Mika, repeating herself.

"Angela was just trying to get to the bottom of all this," I said, as if I'd been calm the whole time.

"He thinks this is a joke," said Angela. "He told me he's a vampire."

"It's the truth," I said.

"Why are you acting like this?" said Mika. "You're being a real asshole."

"I'll prove it," I said to the both of them. "I'll prove that I'm a vampire."

"Oh Jesus," said Angela.

I grabbed Mika by the wrist and motioned for Angela to follow us into the living room. When she didn't budge, I grabbed her too.

"Let go of me," said Angela. I kept my grip tight and didn't loosen up until I'd flung her on to the couch. She fought against me and tried to run for the phone. I grabbed her again, and shoved her back on to the furniture.

"Just sit for a minute," I said.

"You can't tell me what to do," said Angela. "This is my apartment!"

Mika feigned obedience, but I saw fear across her face.

"Where's the remote?" I said. No one responded. So I turned on the television manually. "We're going to sit here until the news comes back on." Ten minutes before, I'd been trying to keep Mika from seeing my face on the TV. But I needed her to watch. It was the only way that she'd believe me.

"What's on the news?" asked Angela.

"Proof," I said, and sat on the couch beside the girls.

Angela moved over to avoid contact with me. "That you're a vampire? Please."

Mika said something under breath, and then again, so that I could hear. "You're being a real piece of shit, David." It hurt, coming from her. But at least she was standing up for herself. I took it as a good sign in the midst of her depression.

"Okay, well..." I tried to change the subject. "Do you want to watch something else? In the meantime?"

***

I sat through two episodes of *Friends* and a made-for-TV-documentary, and fought with Angela several times when she tried to leave her seat. It was my first time holding hostages, and I thought I did okay. I was even able to sneak a call to Fetisynth to book myself a job for the next day.

I needed the job, because I needed the money. And I needed money, because I'd decided – while watching television – that I should go back to Grass Valley and face Daniel. It was the only way to take back some control over my life.

While zoning out, and thinking of what that life could be, I heard Angela's voice.

"Oh my God," she said, and jumped on to the couch with her feet. "Oh my God!"

I looked at the television, and saw what had gotten her so worked up. It was the same clip that had played earlier. The footage from Louis' camcorder. Exactly what I'd hoped for. "See!" I said, and jabbed my finger at the screen.

The girls' reactions were overwhelmingly negative.

"Mika, run!" screamed Angela. She kicked at my head, and then ran for the kitchenette, tripping over herself in a panic.

"You killed Daniel, you fuck!"

I remained with Mika, who'd backed herself into a corner. "Please stop," she said, tearing up for the hundredth time. "You're sick, David. You need help."

"You're right," I said. "I'm sick. I mean, it's something like being sick. I don't know how it works, but I've been told it's in my blood."

"You're not a vampire," said Mika.

"I'm not going to hurt you," I said, and hoped that I'd convinced her. "But you saw the TV, right?"

I heard footsteps behind me, and turned just in time to grab Angela's arm before she impaled me with a steak knife. The speed at which I was able to subdue her surprised me. So did the strength I exhibited when I held her in the air, my hand clasped to her throat.

"Stop it," said Mika. "You're hurting her."

It was hard to reason with Mika while I strangled her friend. But I tried. "Daniel's the one who did this to me. He wants to hurt people. A lot of people. You might be one of them." I could see Angela's face turn blue out of the corner of my eye, so I loosened my grip and let her drop to the floor. "You have to believe me."

Angela clutched her throat and gasped for air.

"See, I'm not trying to hurt anyone." I raised my hands as a symbolic white flag. Still, the girls scrambled away.

Angela ordered Mika to run for the phone. I pleaded, again, for the both of them to listen. But Angela kept fighting me. Mika tried to call the police.

I intervened, because I had to. Because I didn't want to go to prison. And because I couldn't stop Daniel if I was locked away, behind bars. I told myself that I was helping – that I'd make sure no harm would come to Mika. Not from Daniel or any other vampire.

"Don't," I said, and rushed to pull the phone from Mika's hands.

Angela climbed on to my back, and beat at my head and scratched my face. The two continued to attack me until I held them down. They screamed and struggled until I gagged them with pillowcases, and tied their hands and feet with bed sheets and electrical wire.

I apologized over and over. "It's for your own good," I said, and cringed at my words. But I knew that I was right, and that I'd redeem myself one day.

I put Angela in her bedroom, and laid Mika on the couch. No one slept much. But I gave Mika a bedtime story, chock full of my experiences from the past few days. I knew she didn't believe me. Still, I wanted her to have the context, should the facts ever fall in to place. Maybe, one day, Mika would look back on our night together and see it in a different light. I looked forward to that time when I'd no longer be considered a monster.

ONE

A VISION PASSED MY EYES, LIKE A DREAM OF FALSE memories: Mika and Daniel, together, standing on a platform high above me. There was a barrier between us, a viscous film or fog.

My friends held each other in mild embrace. Daniel's hand sat in Mika's. Their bodies merged together at the points of fingers and palms.

Something like jealousy gripped me. I wanted for their touch, but felt weighed down, submerged under the pressure of some ominous force. Or was it so inexplicable? The barrier took on familiar traits as I sunk further into my dream.

I felt a wetness on my skin and sensed that my hair floated around me. My lungs ached for air. I knew that I was drowning.

What were my friends doing above the water's surface? And why did they just watch as I sank into the abyss?

My questions lost their urgency, and I felt a debilitating kind of nausea. It turned my insides sick and told me to give up.

I could see Daniel and Mika, and what they shared at my expense. The message was loud and clear.

I was alone.

FAN-FUCKER

I LEFT MIKA AND ANGELA IN THE MORNING, AND posted notes on the neighbors' doors with polite requests to free the girls from bondage.

Then I went to work.

***

"David!" said the model coordinator as she threw her arms around me. "Thank God you called yesterday. I'd been trying to get a hold of you. Booked you with a super cute girl. She actually requested you."

"Really?"

"Yeah," she said, and changed the subject in an ADHD kind of way. "What happened to your phone?" I had called Fetisynth from Angela's phone, because mine had become lost. "You said it broke? Check this out." The model coordinator handed me her cell, encased in industrial-looking plastic. "I used to crack my screen all the time until I bought this. Now, I'm pretty sure I could run it over with a truck."

"It wasn't the screen," I said.

"Oh," said the model coordinator, as she tapped at the keyboard on her desk. The printer beside her shot out a few sheets of paper. She passed them my way. "You know the drill."

I filled out the paperwork in silence.

"You okay?" asked the model coordinator.

"Yeah," I said. "Why?"

"I don't know. You seem a little off."

"Just tired," I said, which should have been the truth. But I felt unusually well-rested, despite my lack of sleep.

"Well, you better wake up, kid," said said the model coordinator. "Don't want to get wrangled in your sleep."

"I'll be fine," I said between a burgeoning smile. "Really."

"Good to hear," she said, and stole the paper from my fingers. "Have fun."

***

Downstairs, in Fetisynth's production studio, I was escorted to a set, designed to look like a young couple's apartment. The director explained the scenario for the shoot. I was to play a cheating husband, coming home at night with booze and pussy on his breath. My co-star, who I'd had yet to meet, would play my wife. I'd join her in bed, careful not to wake her. But come morning, I'd be tied to the bed posts. She'd grind her pussy across my face and hurl insults at my expense.

The story sounded typical and easy enough. I hoped my mind would be turned off to the nuisance of intellectual process. I wanted to free-float through an endorphin rush of pain and pleasure.

"You're shooting with a new girl today," said the director, Madame Rose. "Goes by the name Lilith. You know her?"

"How would I know her if she's new?" I said.

Madame Rose shrugged. "She seems familiar with you."

"Like, she's seen my porn?"

"You can ask her," said Madame Rose. "She'll be out of makeup in a minute."

As if on cue, I heard the rattle of high heels, like a drum roll to announce the new girls' presence. But she wasn't new. At least, not to me.

Madame Rose greeted her with kind words and smiles. So did the crew. I sat in shock as she walked towards me. She was the vampire I knew as Astrid.

"You know each other?" asked Madame Rose.

Astrid, or Lilith, or whatever she wanted to be called, took one look at me and told a bold-faced lie. "No, I don't think so. But I'm a fan of your work." She extended her hand. "Nice to meet you."

I glanced towards Madame Rose, as if she might see the worry in my head. But all she did was make a face, like she thought I was being rude. So I shook Astrid's hand and let out a robotic response. "You too."

Madame Rose cut the moment short. "Let's get started." She looked me over. "David, what you're wearing is fine. Lilith, do you have a bra and panty combo? If not, you can just be naked. You're supposed to be asleep for the intro. I know I sleep naked."

"Me too," said Astrid. She peeled back her latex dress. Slowly. It looked like she was doing a kind of striptease.

I didn't understand Astrid's motivation for facing me on a porn set. Did she plan to dominate me into joining her vampire revolution? Or did she think that she could seduce me into changing my mind? Surely, there was a reason I'd yet to figure out.

"David," said Madame Rose. "Stand outside the door and peek your head in. Like you're checking to make sure that she's asleep. Lilith, get into bed. Close your eyes. Find a natural position, so you don't look like a mannequin."

Astrid and I took our places. We froze for the flashes of

the still camera, and continued on to the next instructed act. Eventually, we found ourselves together under the sheets. We faced opposite directions, acting out the sleeping habits of an estranged husband and wife.

"David," said Astrid, in a whisper.

"What are you doing here?" I asked.

"You're important to us," said Astrid. "It upsets me to think you may have gotten the wrong impression."

"This is beyond inappropriate," I said, as if I'd retained some moral high-ground.

"Please stop talking," barked Madame Rose. "I'm seeing all of these awkward photos with your mouths open." She ran her fingers along her lips, like she'd zipped them up.

"Sorry," I said, and reverted back to my porno act. Flashes of light burst from the photo camera. Then we started the sequence over for video. I tip-toed into the room, slipped out of my clothes, and nestled myself beneath the sheets. Astrid remained still, as if she were asleep.

"Perfect," said Madame Rose. "Now let's get you tied up." She shuffled towards me with an arm full of rope, and bound my wrists and ankles to the corners of the bed.

Astrid crawled across me and straddled my chest. "Isn't he cute?" she said, so that everyone could hear.

"Dreamy," said Madame Rose, who shook her head right after. "Now grind your pussy on his face, and tell him how worthless he is. Work your magic."

Astrid rested her face against my cheek. "Is there anything I should know?" she whispered.

"About what?" I asked.

"What you're into," she said. "What gets you off?"

I couldn't believe what I was hearing. "Are you fucking serious?"

"Action," said Madame Rose.

Astrid picked herself up and dropped back down over my face. I was suffocated by her labia. "You think you can do what you want?" she said. "Come home when you want? What about my needs? Did you ever think about bringing home one of your whore girlfriends? Or are you out with other men? Is that it? Am I not good enough without a cock?" Astrid spit on my face and slapped me across my thighs, and then crawled towards a dresser that had been staged near the bed. She pulled out a harnessed, eight-inch dildo from the bottom drawer. "Big enough for you?" She rubbed the synthetic shaft across my lips.

Madame Rose clapped her hands, and said, "Great. This is perfect for a transition."

"Yeah?" Astrid's demeanor changed to polite and bubbly. "Did I do okay?"

"You were fine, sweetheart. Take five. We need to get David ready for the next scene." Madame Rose tended to the knots around my limbs, and asked if I needed some time to stretch myself out. I nodded. She called for a production assistant, and asked him to fetch me a bottle of lube and a butt plug.

***

The studio had been converted from an old military bunker, and so the bathrooms were large and open, and had several rows of toilet stalls. I hid in the stall furthest from the door, and rinsed out my ass with a disposable enema.

"David?" said Astrid, from somewhere near the entrance.

I didn't answer.

"David, you don't have to hide." I heard her footsteps turn loud before they stopped right in front of me. The stall door became the only barrier between us.

It seemed silly to pretend that I wasn't there or couldn't hear her. "I'm not hiding," I said. "Just cleaning out. So I won't shit on you."

My explanation didn't dissuade her from conversation. "I'm sorry that I scared you off. When you were in my home."

"You didn't scare me," I said.

"It's a lot to take in," said Astrid, as if to comfort me. "The story of God and our creation."

"If it makes you feel better, it sounded just as stupid as any other religious bullshit."

Astrid placed her hands against the stall. I could see the tips of her feet beneath the door. "There's something Daniel once told me. It must have happened around the time you two became, well, lovers. Your parents forced you to see a counselor. A Christian one. Do you remember?"

Of course, I remembered. It happened to me, to Daniel, to us – a thorn in the side of our early romance. It didn't sit right with me that Astrid should know about it. It should have been mine. Daniel's. What right did she have to access my old life?

CONFUSED

MY PARENTS WEREN'T DEVOTED ENOUGH TO make it a weekly routine. But when they felt the need, we attended a small community church – a non-denominational sect of Christian fundamentalists, evangelicals, and roof-raising speakers of tongues.

Daniel and I were put in Sunday school on the days that religion beckoned our family. There, we learned the stories of Noah's ark, the parting of the Red Sea, and the birth, death, and resurrection of Jesus Christ. The stories never took on a personal significance, because they were delivered as fact. I just came to think of the past as a fantastical place that had lost its magic along the way.

Later, around puberty, I found music that mocked Christianity and books that explained the world outside of a religious lens. Mostly, I was interested in the works that refuted what my parents had once told me. God became a thing, to me, that old people believed in. I settled on the notion that science had explained away all need for faith.

After a while, the efforts to get me to church became too great for my mother. My father didn't care much either way.

But Daniel's parents and mine both agreed on an intervention when they'd discovered our first kiss. One of their tactics involved a youth pastor named Robert Michaels. My mother drove us to the church we'd attended as children, and left us alone with Robert for what seemed like several hours. Daniel and I were separated on opposite sides of the his small office, as if the distance would remove any chance of our affection.

"I want you both to know this is a safe place," said Robert. "I'm not trying to pass judgement, or anything like that."

"Then why are we here?" said Daniel.

Robert smiled and leaned back in his chair. "I'd say it's because your parents are worried about you guys. I mean, come on. They're parents. It's their job to be worried."

Daniel and I both shrugged, but only to promote our appearance as disaffected youth. It seemed that Robert took our gesture as a sign of opening up. "I'm just here to help you out," he continued. "I was a kid once too. I know what it's like. You're going through a lot of changes. Things can be confusing."

"We know why we're here," I said.

"Yeah? Why's that?"

"We're not stupid," I said. "They don't want us to be gay. You're supposed to fix us."

"That's a reasonable concern for a parent," said Robert. "Don't you think?

Daniel yawned. "Well, they fucked up bringing us here. You're obviously a faggot."

Robert froze, as if in shock, and let out a small laugh. After a moment, he said, "Oh, come on, guys. I'm not what you said. And let's be real for a minute. Neither are you." He flung a hand across his desk and swiped up a Bible. "Look, God loves you. It's written right here, in this book."

"Yeah?" said Daniel. "What page is that on?"

Robert ignored the question. "But God's set up some rules.

They can have pretty harsh consequences if you don't follow them." He flipped the book open to somewhere near the beginning. "Now, in Genesis 13:13, we have the first mention of the men of Sodom. Have you ever heard of the word sodomy? It means sex in the..." He mouthed the word butt, as if it were a crime to say out loud. "Gross, right? That word comes from this place called Sodom. Genesis says the men who lived in Sodom *'were wicked and sinners before the Lord exceedingly.'* Their story is continued in chapters 18 and 19 with their sin being so great that, not only does God say it is *'very grievous,'* but He comes down to destroy them with fire. The rubble still stands as a warning for us today.

"What was their sin, you might ask?" said Robert. "It was *'lying with mankind as with womankind.'* Now, what do you think that means?"

Neither Daniel nor I would answer him.

"Lying down with a man," said Robert, while making quotes with his fingers, "sounds a lot like sodomy. Like homosexuality."

"What about just rimming?" said Daniel. "Is that okay?"

I laughed and played along. "Or felching?"

"I'm not going to pretend that I know what either of those things mean," said Robert. "But let's not forget that sodomy is the only sin God came down from Heaven to destroy. He's dealt with other stuff in other ways. But He rained down fire for sodomy."

"This girl in my math class told me that she only has anal sex, because she's saving her real virginity," I said. "She's Catholic. But isn't that also sodomy?"

Robert squeezed his eyes shut, as if to dispel the image from his head. "You're missing the point," he said. "It's lying with mankind that's a sin."

"She was talking about having sex with guys," I said.

"No," said Robert. "I mean, men lying with men. Even in the New Testament, this is declared to be *'against nature.'* The apostle, Paul, says in Romans 1 that *'men leave the natural use of woman.'* There is no greater sin against God than to reject how He made you."

"What if God made me a sodomizer?" said Daniel.

"That's ridiculous," said Robert. "Why would God make someone that He, in His own words, would describe as wicked and sinful? If that were the case, and you were born a sodomite, you'd just be a walking, talking abomination. So come on, you guys. You're not a couple of sinful abominations, right? You're just confused."

GIVING IN

"DANIEL DOESN'T LIE TO ME," SAID ASTRID. "SO I'M sure that it happened. I'm just not sure whether it had as much of an impact on you."

"I assure you that frumpy, little man didn't fuck up Daniel," I said. "Not in any significant way."

"You were children," said Astrid. "Words can have a profound effect on young people. Even if that man didn't hurt you, think of the rest of the world; all the children who will sit before pastors and priests, and be spoon-fed guilt. And for what? So that they might spend an eternity with God?"

Astrid kicked in the stall door. I was still naked and sitting on the toilet. She was back-lit and looked like a silhouette. Her arms were spread just enough to give her the appearance of an angel, fallen or ascended.

"We have the power to give those same children eternal life," said Astrid. "You witnessed Daniel come back from the dead. You know what's possible. I don't want your anger towards me to stop you from doing something great." Astrid knelt before me, and raised her hands, like in a prayer. "This is my apology. My plea for forgiveness. Join us. Please. Raise our army."

I was moved by her gesture, and so considered what she'd said.

She has a point. At least some children would be spared a life of guilt.

But who are you to force people to change their lives, to become vampires?

If they know what they're getting into, it might not be so bad.

No one is going to let you bite them, or listen to you talk about why they should.

Whatever. I don't care. I'll just tell her what she wants to hear, so that she'll get off my back. I'm withholding responsibility for everything that follows.

That's not how it works.

Shut up.

"Okay," I said to Astrid, who was still on her knees. "I'm not angry. This is just really weird. Like, you being here."

"I know," said Astrid. "Though, I'd hoped your ability to accept the unorthodox had changed. In light of recent events. And I didn't know where else I'd have the chance to talk to you, one on one."

The last of the enema poured from my ass. There was a splash of water, louder than I'd hoped for. "Maybe I could have a minute to myself," I said. "See you on set?"

"Consider what I've said. If not for me, then for Daniel."

"I'm considering," I said.

She stood and turned to leave. But before she'd exited the bathroom, Astrid said, "Could I at least drive you to meet him?"

"Who? Daniel?"

"Yes."

"In Grass Valley?"

Again, Astrid said, "Yes."

There seemed no point in arguing, so I said, "I'll think about it."

A silence followed. There were no footsteps, so I knew that she was still nearby. "Don't think badly of me," said Astrid. "I've never done this before."

"What?" I asked.

"What we're about to do."

"You mean you've never fucked a guy in the ass before?"

"I haven't," she said, embarrassed.

Inside my head, I couldn't wait for it all to be over. But I told Astrid, "I'm sure you'll be fine."

***

Astrid whipped, fucked, and belittled me, and all with an air of hesitation. Normally, I would have taken her act as a sign of inexperience. But she was careful more than crude. She removed the leather hood from my face, and I began to understand why.

I saw the way she looked at me. I was more to her than a piece of meat. She couldn't even pretend otherwise. To her, I was the leader Daniel spoke of: her bound and beaten god.

A LINEAGE

I AGREED TO LET ASTRID DRIVE ME BACK TO Grass Valley. It was hard to refuse her after she'd spent so much time worshipping my erection. In fact, it was hard to refuse her, period.

I had no means of driving myself. My car was still in Santa Cruz. And I didn't want to use public transportation. Not with my face plastered all over the news.

Astrid's offer was the best I had. So I leaned back in her Honda Civic and closed my eyes; relaxed for the first time since Daniel had put his teeth in me.

***

Somewhere along Interstate 80, Astrid flipped on the radio. The sounds of classical orchestration filled the car. Astrid must have sensed that I was awake, because she said, "I saw him perform once."

"Who?" I asked, from my half-slumber.

"Beethoven. Not this piece, I don't think. But it was beautiful."

"You're fucking with me, right?"

"My friends and I would sneak into the rafters of the concert house in Vienna."

"You're from Austria?"

"It's where I was born," said Astrid.

"Wait," I said, and grabbed the lever beneath my seat until I was upright. "How old are you?"

She took moment to think it over. "Two hundred fifteen. Maybe two hundred eighteen. Twenty? Funny, I've lost track."

"Whoa," I said. "You must have seen some shit in your lifetime."

"Yeah," said Astrid, as if lost in her own memories.

"So can I ask the big question?"

"What question is that?"

"You know," I said. "How did you become a vampire?"

"Me?"

"Unless you don't want to say."

"No," said Astrid. "There should be no secrets between us." She turned off the radio, and stared at the open road for what seemed like several minutes. "Like I said, I was born in Vienna. I believe in 1793. There weren't birth certificates back then for people like me. My mother worked in a brothel, and I didn't know my father. He was likely a man who'd paid to have my mother for a night.

"My mother was pregnant when she died. The baby was lost with her. I was put into the brothel's care, and forced to work when I turned twelve."

"When you say work, you mean as a hooker?" I asked, somewhat shocked.

"We're not so different, you and I," said Astrid, with a coy smile. "Except that what I did wasn't always safe. Wasn't always fun."

"Porn isn't *always* fun," I said, as if to make the claim that I worked hard too.

"Have you ever sucked a penis that wasn't washed in two weeks?" said Astrid.

"That's fucking disgusting," I said. "And I get your point."

"I was, maybe, seventeen when I became sick. Sores broke out all over me. I lost more weight than any girl should. Every joint in my body was on fire. It was probably Syphilis, but no one knew about diseases like that when I was young.

"Of course, men wouldn't pay to sleep with me. I had no money. No food. Soon, I was out on the streets. I thought it was the end for me.

"One night, a man approached me in the dark. I thought that, perhaps, he hadn't seen my sores. I threw myself at him, and kissed and groped his waist.

"Sure enough, he wanted my body, but not for what I'd thought."

"He was a vampire?" I asked.

Astrid nodded. "In hindsight, I can only guess that he'd meant to eat me. He pulled me into an alley and covered my mouth. I didn't struggle much. Didn't even have the strength to scream. When he bit into my flesh, I froze. Maybe I'd given myself over to death.

"But a couple of men stumbled upon us. They looked like police of some sort. The men raised clubs and hurried towards us. It was enough to scare the vampire away."

"That's it?" I asked, when Astrid's tale turned to silence.

"The vampire saved my life," she said.

"Because you were healed?" I said. "Of Syphilis, or whatever?"

"And of everything since."

"Then you moved to Oregon, end of story, huh?"

"I live in San Francisco" she said, as if to mock me. "You

asked how I became a vampire, and I told you. If there's more you want to know..."

"Forget it," I said.

"Well, what about you?"

"What about me?"

"Tell me something I wouldn't have heard from Daniel," said Astrid.

"Okay. You want, like, first date answers?" I said. "I've never left the country. My favorite food is, or was, Americanized Chinese food. I've been going to school to learn how to make movies, but I guess that's never going to happen."

"You don't know that," said Astrid.

"Your turn," I said, to take the focus off of me.

"Again?" she said, and took her time to pick another story. "I came to America because of love."

"I'm listening," I said.

"You know what it's like to change," said Astrid. "What it's like when there's no one to tell you what's happening. I was scared. I had a hunger I couldn't control.

"Soon after I was bitten, there were rumors of a monster in the Vienna slums. Vigilante groups sprung up to hunt me down.

"I fled, of course. Headed northwest through the states of modern Germany. Years passed, and I still looked like a young woman. The same as I do now.

"I never stayed in one place for long. So I always felt a kind of loneliness. I'd spend time, when I was able, at universities – around those who looked the same age as me. I wasn't an intellectual. But I loved listening to the students. In the 1820's, there was talk of taxation, political censorship, and so forth. The students spoke of national unity and democracy. It all seemed very exciting.

"I met a boy named Gottfried at the university in Heidelberg. He was the first to approach me since I was a teenager in Vienna. The first to show an interest, anyway. We talked for hours on our first night together. After that, we were inseparable.

"It was hard in the beginning. Whenever we kissed or made love, I felt an urge to drink his blood. I'd often sneak away while he slept, so that I could find nourishment for myself. But I made our relationship work until he graduated. He never suspected a thing.

"Then Gottfried got his hands on a manuscript that praised a country across the Atlantic for its plentiful harvests and intellectual freedom. It put the idea in his head to go to America. He wanted us both to move there."

I interrupted. "So it's possible to date someone who's not a vampire? For them to never know?"

Astrid shook her head. "Possible? Maybe. In my experience, it doesn't last.

"I wanted to go to America with Gottfried. But I didn't think about the consequences. We traveled by sea. I was trapped on a ship, and with nowhere to hide. You understand?"

I nodded.

"I tried not to eat for a week. My skin turned pale and I lost my strength. Gottfried thought that I'd grown ill, and even believed that I would die. I was in love with him. How could I let him suffer like that?

"One night, I crept away while he was sleeping. I searched for someone who was traveling alone. Someone who wouldn't be missed. Near the far end of the ship, I found a man who slept apart from all the others. I broke his neck and bled him dry.

"I tried to be quick and quiet. But I managed to wake a little girl. She saw the blood on the man's neck and around my mouth, and started screaming. The whole ship woke to find me kneeling over a corpse.

"And Gottfried..." Astrid's lips began to quiver. Her eyes became wet.

I felt wrong to continue watching her. It was like I'd become a voyeur without the eroticism, an exploiter of failed dreams. I turned my attention to the dashboard and to the blurred pavement outside the window.

"Sorry," said Astrid. She wiped a hand across her face.

She turned the radio back on. The speakers blared some synth rock band. Astrid nodded her head to the beat. "I saw this band too," she said. "Just last week. Beethoven's fine. But concerts these days are more fun, don't you think?"

A HOME IN THE NORTH

IT WAS DARK WHEN WE ARRIVED IN GRASS Valley. Darker by the time we passed on to the neighboring town, Nevada City. Astrid said that Daniel had checked into a hotel in the area.

I looked around me, beyond the rural roads, and felt my childhood disappear. I'd once thought of my hometown as the last innocent place on earth. Maybe because of Daniel; because I'd fallen in love with him there. When I'd moved away, I still thought of it as a land outside of time – preserved by some magic that Daniel and I had left there. But the magic was nowhere to be seen. Instead, there were bits of construction, strip malls, Starbucks, and a Walmart. My fairytale village had become a bland, commercial jungle.

At least the hotel lacked the appearance of renovation. The paint looked cracked and the wooden beams sagged.

We pulled into the parking lot, which was still half-gravel, and walked to a room on the first floor. Astrid knocked. I stood back and tilted my head, intoxicated by the smell of cedar, pine, and smoke from a nearby chimney.

Daniel answered the door. He wore nothing but a pair of slim-fitting sweatpants that hung low on his waist. He hugged Astrid, and smiled at me with his head on her shoulder. "Glad you could make it," he said.

"Of course," said Astrid.

I remained still, and with my hands stuffed in my pockets. Daniel let Astrid inside, and then lingered by the door. "It's cold out," he said, even though the weather was warm.

I couldn't define my hesitation. Sure, Daniel and I hadn't parted on the best of terms. But there was something else holding me back.

Not long before, I'd believed my whole life was ahead of me. There were infinite possibilities in the words, "When I grow up." But to grow old was no longer an option. Through the door, where Daniel stood, the possibilities became so few. Standing my ground felt like the last protest I had to the grips of fate.

I closed my eyes, so that I might have stayed within my fleeting state of indecision. But I couldn't block out the sounds: the crunch of Daniel's footsteps, the wind he exhaled over my face, or the words he whispered as he wrapped his arms around me. "I missed you," he said.

"Yeah?"

"I'd almost forgotten how much you fuck me up. I mean, in a 'I can't stop thinking about you' kind of way."

I felt Daniel breath up my scent.

"I begged Astrid to bring you here," said Daniel. "What we're going to do... I can't do it without you."

What he said wasn't important. It was the way his fingers hit my flesh. He made me feel like I was fifteen all over again. "Uh huh," I said, as he guided me inside the hotel room and on to his bed. I pretended that we were home, and that all had returned to normal. For a moment, it felt true.

Before I fell asleep, I heard Astrid say, "He's just tired, Daniel. He's had a long day."

“He’s beautiful when he’s sleeping,” said Daniel.

I meant to say it back, but it was too late to get the words out: You’re beautiful too.

WE RETRACE OUR STEPS

THE MORNING CAME WITH THE SMELL OF coffee, eggs, pastries, and something else. I was the first one to bed and the last to wake up. Daniel and Astrid were already seated at the table in the corner of the room, forking down their continental breakfast with their favorite condiment, human blood.

"Rest well?" said Astrid.

I rubbed the Sandman from my eyes. "What time is it?"

"A little after ten," said Daniel. "Want to go for a walk?"

"Now?"

He shrugged. "After you eat and shower."

"Sure," I said, and shuffled towards the bathroom. I turned on the water and let it wash my naked skin.

Where do you think Daniel wants to go on our walk?

There aren't a lot of options in this town. Every path leads to nowhere.

What are you going to do about the rest of it? The vampire crusades and all?

Why do I have to do anything?

Because that's why you're here. To do something. To stop it, or...

I shouldn't have to worry. Nothing comes of anything that starts in this place, this town. I mean, look at me.

What if you're wrong? You told Mika that you were the good guy. That means you have to act.

Does it, though?

The shower went cold, and I traded my thoughts for a towel. I stepped out and looked in the mirror. My reflection was fogged, and I appeared as someone else. Maybe a man with the courage to open the door – to do a lot more.

Daniel waited for me on the bed. He tossed me an unopened package of blood. "Drink this. It's better than the shit they're serving here."

I did as he instructed. "Where are we going?"

Astrid made a suggestion. "You should show me around. Downtown, your old school, anything you think is worth seeing."

"Wait," I said. "If we go to the school, we're not..."

"Relax," said Daniel. "It would just be to look around. A visit. We could check in on old Mrs. Stample. See if she's still alive."

"There's so much of your history here," said Astrid. "I want to get a taste of it. Before we change everything."

***

Downtown Nevada City was comprised of two streets, side by side. Its shops and restaurants were built on the skeletons of an old mining town. After time spent away, it looked somehow unreal, like the street facades at Disneyland. Astrid said that it reminded her of when she first moved out West. Except the buildings were brighter and more colorful.

Daniel acted as our tour guide. He pointed out the market where we used to steal beer and the alley where we'd get stoned during the annual street parades. I was nearly caught up in the nostalgia. But a hurt in my chest overshadowed it all.

Every anecdote Daniel brought up, spoke aloud to Astrid, reminded me of what I'd lost. I wanted to live our childhood all over again; to kiss Daniel's face and never let him go.

Daniel didn't look a day older than when he'd left. Still sixteen and perfect. Exactly like the boy who broke my heart. In a way, he was doing it all over again. I might have forgiven him if he just acted like he used to. Even if he'd just hold my fucking hand.

Astrid brought me out of my self-pity. "I'm thirsty," she said. "Not for blood, though. Something sweet."

"Should we take her to Mekka?" asked Daniel.

"What's Mekka?" said Astrid.

"The only trendy coffee shop around here," I said.

"You think that boy, Nick, still works there?" said Daniel.

"Who?"

"The cute one," said Daniel.

It felt like he was twisting a knife in my chest. Daniel and Astrid both stared at me as if I'd become ill.

"The coffee shop," said Astrid. "It's just over that way, right?"

"Yeah. We'll catch up with you in a minute." Daniel motioned for Astrid to go on ahead of us.

When she was out of site, Daniel pushed me down; forced me to sit on the sidewalk curb. "I know something's wrong," he said. "You can't hide that shit from me."

"It's kind of a mindfuck being back here," I said. "With you."

"I know, right?" Daniel seemed to agree, but on his own terms.

"I can't not think about, you know... before."

"So what do you want?" asked Daniel. "For things to be the

way they used to?"

I shrugged. "Maybe."

"So do I," he said, and sat beside me.

"Shit isn't the same. It's never going to be."

"Why not?" Daniel tried to grab at my crotch. "I don't still make you hard?"

"Fuck you," I said, and pushed his hand away.

"No, fuck you," he said. "I'm sorry. I'm sorry. I'm sorry. Okay? You think this isn't weird for me too? I know everything's still fucked up for you. But I basically let you kill me. Twice. What's that if not... I mean, you want me to say it?"

"Say what?"

"Fine," said Daniel. "I still love you."

"That's heavy."

"That's all you have to say?"

"No," I said, and tried my best to keep it together. "But you've never said that to me before."

"I'm saying it now."

"I love you," I said. "Like, I think I'm in love with you. Still."

"That's what I meant," said Daniel.

"Okay."

We sat in awkward anticipation, reminiscent of the moments before we'd first tasted each other's lips.

Then it happened. Daniel kissed me again. I held his face near mine, and kept him there as long as possible.

***

Astrid was in the back corner booth of Cafe Mekka. She sipped from a slushy, fruit drink and stared at her phone. We approached her, hand in hand.

She raised her head. "You two are adorable."

"If you say so." Daniel smiled at me.

"Everything okay?" asked Astrid.

I nodded.

"Good," she said. "So what now?"

"Unfortunately, you've seen the entire downtown area in the span of, what..."

"Two hours," I said. "Sorry. This place can be underwhelming."

"It won't be that way for long," said Astrid. "In ten years' time, people will look back here and say, 'This is where it all started. They had the courage to stand up to God.'"

Just when things were going well, she had to bring it up.

"Maybe don't talk about that in public," said Daniel. "Not yet. People are going to think you're crazy."

"I'm sorry," said Astrid. "But it's exciting. When do I get to see your school?"

"We could go now," said Daniel. "If you want."

"Sure," I said, and meant the opposite.

THE YOUTH

"IT WON'T BE THE END OF THEIR EDUCATION," said Astrid. "If that's what you're worried about."

We stood on a hill, overlooking Seven Hills Middle School – a landscape of boxy classrooms, fields, asphalt, and a small gymnasium. Astrid must have noticed my hesitation to descend into the valley of institutionalized education. But her attempts to move me along came out of left field.

"It would be a hiatus at most," she said. "If vampirism spreads as quickly as I think it will, we'll have to become an acknowledged part of society. Children will bite their parents. Then the parents will bite their spouses, colleagues, friends..."

"Or kill them," I said. "I didn't just bite someone. I murdered him."

"Because we didn't get to you in time," said Astrid. "No one explained what was happening to you."

"Who will explain to these kids?" I said.

"You and Daniel, of course," she said. "Me, if I need to."

"If we don't get to them in time?"

Astrid shrugged. "A little killing's not so bad."

"We'll make sure to do it right," said Daniel, with a hand placed on my shoulder.

"Why now?" I said, to Astrid. "Why didn't you start changing them before?"

"Daniel said it wasn't time."

"What about before you met him?" I said. "You could have done this a long time ago."

"Before Daniel came along, we didn't think it was possible."

Daniel grabbed me by the arm and pulled me down the embankment, towards the school. He nearly ran, and I went with him. Soon enough, we were several yards ahead of Astrid.

"You've brainwashed that girl," I said.

"I haven't," said Daniel. "She had a role for me to fill. I've just become what she wanted me to be."

"What about what I want?"

Astrid caught up and nearly squeezed herself between us. "You two keeping secrets?" she asked.

"No secrets," said Daniel. He stared me down, as if to force an agreement.

I said nothing, but felt that my gut had turned sick.

"Okay," said Astrid. She sounded unconvinced.

A wave of interference washed away the mounting tension. It was a high-pitched squeal that reached us all at once. I looked towards the sound, and saw a plump, middle-aged woman marching towards us. She had a whistle between her lips, and dropped it to say, "This is school property. You need to leave immediately. Otherwise, I'll be forced to contact the authorities."

"We're visiting," said Daniel.

"Visiting?" said the woman. She examined our bodies for an uncomfortable amount of time. Finally, she turned her attention back to our faces. "I don't see any badges."

"Badges?" said Astrid.

"Your visitor's badges," said the woman.

"We used to be students here," said Daniel.

"I don't recognize a one of you," said the woman. "And I've worked this school for five years."

"It was more like eight years ago," I said.

"Who are you visiting?" asked the woman. She'd dropped the accusatory tone, but still sounded bitter. I couldn't imagine what it was like to be a student on her bad side.

"Mrs. Stample?" said Daniel. "She still teaches here, right?"

The woman scratched her head. "I'm going to have to escort you to the main office. To get your badges." She pointed in the direction of the building, and forced us to lead the way. It seemed like another sign of her suspicion – to make sure we knew where we were going.

Both Daniel and I remembered where the front desk was, but we couldn't piece together the woman's role in getting us there. Astrid was the only one brave enough to ask. "So what is it that you do here?"

"Me?" said the woman, as if the answer was obvious. "I'm a yard duty."

"What's that?" said Astrid.

"You didn't have yard duties when you were in school?" said the woman. "I keep the kids in line during recess and while they're milling about between classes. No one ditches school on my watch. And no strangers come waltzing in her. Not to vandalize or anything else."

***

We arrived at the front office. Despite the yard duty's claims that we were hooligans, the school secretary gave us badges – white stickers with our names scrawled out – and welcomed us back to Seven Hills. Then we were allowed to check in on Mrs. Stample's class.

The yard duty insisted that she show us the way. She opened

the classroom door and interrupted a room full of sixth grade students. "I hate to barge in here," she said. "But these three insisted on making a visit. The office says it's okay. So what can I do?"

Mrs. Stample took one look at us and said, "Look who we have here!" She batted away the yard duty, and embraced Daniel and me. Though, when she put her arms around Astrid, she said, "Oh dear, forgive me. Were you in my class?"

"No," said Astrid. "I'm just a friend. From the Bay Area."

"It's okay to leave them here?" said the yard duty.

"Yes, of course," said Mrs. Stample, who held the door open for the yard duty and shut it firmly behind her.

We turned to face the twenty-odd students peering up at us from their desks.

"Sorry, class," said Mrs. Stample. "Sorry for the distraction. Return to your tests. I'll give you an extra five minutes to finish. After, we'll get to talk to our special guests here."

Mrs. Stample continued to speak to us in an unrestrained whisper. "You don't mind, do you? Talking to the kids a bit? I'm sure they'd get a kick out of it." Then, as if on second thought, she said, "Actually..." She motioned for us to leave the room with her.

Once outside, Mrs. Stample said, "Can I ask what you're up to these days? Are you working, at a university, or anything like that?"

"I'm in film school," I said, before Daniel or Astrid could ruin our visit with a more inappropriate truth. "And..."

"Astrid and I work in the medical field," said Daniel, much to my relief.

"That's great," said Mrs. Stample. "I'm so proud of you boys. You too, Astrid. I was just asking, because... How do I put this?

I want my past students to be a good influence on the current ones."

We all muttered something to convey our understanding.

"I always knew you two would go on to do something great. A good teacher can always tell." I didn't buy it. If I'd been on a path to greatness, it was no longer the case. Either Mrs. Stample's brilliance detector had waned with age, or she was full of shit.

I assumed the latter, because she seemed capable enough of remembering the past. "Daniel," she said, after some deliberation. "I read in the papers, years ago, that you had, well, died. Obviously, that's not the case. But something happened?"

"Not really," said Daniel. "It was a very temporary, teenage-run-away-type-of-thing."

"Of course," said Mrs. Stample. "I just remember it being a bigger deal than that."

"It's Nevada County," I said, covering for Daniel. "Everything is made to be a bigger deal than it is."

"I suppose you're right," said Mrs. Stample. "In any case, it's good to see you. What brings you back here? I should have asked when you first walked through the door."

"We're..."

"...Visiting."

"...And I wanted to see their school."

It made sense that college-aged people might return to their hometown, and so there were no questions as to the validity of what we'd said.

We re-entered the classroom. The students finished their tests and stacked their papers on a podium near the chalkboard.

Mrs. Stample's post-test routine was the same as I remembered. She asked the students to return to their seats, and inspected each desk, individually.

When I was her pupil, she'd looked for scratch paper, note cards, or anything else that we could have used to cheat. In the time since, students had come into possession of cell phones, tablets, and other electronic devices. Mrs. Stample found one hidden within a young girl's desk.

"What do we have here?" said Mrs. Stample.

The girl's cheeks turned red. "I'm sorry."

"You know the rule about phones," said Mrs. Stample.

"I do," said the girl, and she added another, "Sorry."

The phone vibrated in Mrs. Stamples hands, and the screen lit up. "Oh, and we're texting in class? Who is Bradxxx2000?"

"I don't know." The girl stared at the floor. She looked like she was going to cry.

"He must be acquainted. Because he wants you to know that you're, spelled UR, cute and then the number 2."

"I..."

"There's no need for excuses, young lady," said Mrs. Stample. "You're going in the closet."

The remaining students straightened up. They looked to the front of the class, like a swarm of shivering robots. The girl didn't move. Not until Mrs. Stample grabbed her arm and dragged her to the back of the room. She opened a small door and shoved the girl inside; pushed a chair up under the handle to keep the girl from fleeing.

It took barely a moment for Mrs. Stample to regain her composure. She smiled at us, and continued to check the students' desks.

I sensed, from the look on Daniel and Astrid's faces, that they were as appalled as I was. Thoughts poured through my mind, each a way to intervene. But I wasn't sure if I'd witnessed actual corporal punishment or something still allowed in contemporary public schools. Minutes passed. I couldn't believe that I'd grown to be such a passive wretch. But I did nothing to help the girl. Neither did anyone else.

"As you may have noticed," said Mrs. Stample, addressing her students, "we have some visitors. And guess what? They used to sit right where you are now." She presented us as if we were a prize on an old game show. Like she should have said, "Look! You could turn into one of these." It was exactly what Daniel and Astrid would have liked them to believe.

"I'm Daniel, and this is David. We used to be Seven Hills students. So I guess we know what it's like. Things get better. I promise." Daniel let out an awkward laugh. "Oh, and this is our friend, Astrid."

Astrid raised her hand to acknowledge her presence.

"Why don't you tell them what you do?" said Mrs. Stample. She couldn't seem to help herself, and answered for him, even though she was mistaken. "He's a doctor."

"Actually, no," said Daniel, which seemed to irritate Mrs. Stample. "I do work in the medical industry, but not as a doctor."

"Oh?"

"I work with organs and blood," said Daniel. "I transport them to hospitals and other facilities."

I didn't realize that our visit would turn into a career day. Mrs. Stample pressed Daniel with questions until he'd given a somewhat thorough explanation of how an organ was taken from a corpse and given to a patient, who needed it to live.

Next, she gave me the drill. But I was shy and bad at public speaking. By the time I'd finished, I was sure that I'd dissuaded her entire class from going to college.

Eventually, the bell rang. The children rushed for the door. I attempted to join the herd of eager students, but stopped when I noticed the chair still tucked beneath the closet door handle.

Mrs. Stample seemed distracted by the papers on her desk. So I called out to her. "Don't you think it's time to let the girl out?"

"She's aware that she'll be spending some after-school time in there too."

"Oh," I said.

CATCH AND RELEASE

ASTRID ENCOURAGED MY ANGER. SHE SAID, "Yes," and, "I know," and so many other phrases that insisted she agreed with me.

"I understand it's not the worst you can do to a kid," I said. "I mean, she didn't hit the girl. But come on."

Astrid continued her mantra.

"It has to be against school policy for a teacher to do something like that."

"What if it's not?" said Daniel.

"She locked that girl in the closet, and right in front of us," I said. "Like it was no big deal. Like she couldn't possibly get in trouble. All the girl did was text a boy. What the fuck is wrong with that?"

"I don't think there's anything wrong with that," said Astrid.

"Did she ever do anything like that to us?" I asked Daniel.

"I don't know," said Daniel. "There was other stuff for sure. It was sixth grade. When you got in trouble, it sucked."

"All the more reason to put a stop to it," said Astrid.

"What do you mean?"

"You and Daniel would never abuse children, would you?"

"Yeah, but..." I stopped about a block from where the buses lined up outside the school. A throng of students passed us by. I didn't want them to overhear Astrid's transformation cult conspiracy. "What exactly do we plan on doing? I get the part where we bite the kids. But then we have to explain to each one, individually, what's happening to them? And tell them that they should refrain from bleeding each other to death? Are we supposed to start our own vampire school, or what?"

"Daniel has the answer," said Astrid.

"So what is it?"

Daniel put a finger to his lips, the universal sign for us to shut up. He nodded towards two approaching boys.

The taller boy said, "You were just in Mrs. Stample's class, right?"

Daniel nodded, yes.

"Your job sounds pretty gross," said the shorter boy. "You really have to touch people's kidneys and stuff?"

"I really do," said Daniel.

"Do you have any here?" asked the taller boy.

Daniel looked like he was about to say, "Sorry." But he reconsidered. "I might," he said, and looked to Astrid, as if he'd passed her some silent bit of information. "You wouldn't want to see it, would you?"

"It's from a real person?" said the shorter boy.

"Gross," said the taller boy. "But fuck yeah."

"Come with us," said Daniel. "We'll show you."

"We're staying at the Bridled Goose hotel," said Astrid. "The walk from here isn't bad."

"Um, Daniel." I raised my hand, like I was back in school. But Daniel didn't call on me. He just moved us along, and tended to the boys like they were his favored pupils.

I began to see what was happening, but couldn't figure out the details. Maybe that was the problem. There were no details.

Astrid was in the dark about how her prophecy would be fulfilled, and Daniel made every effort to keep it that way. Bringing two boys back to our hotel might have been his only chance at convincing someone, anyone, to become a vampire. But it wasn't his plan. The boys had happened upon us by coincidence.

What could I do? Tell the kids of their possible fate? I couldn't convince Mika that I was a vampire. I doubted that I'd fair better with twelve-year-old strangers. But I'd told Mika that I was the good guy. How could I follow through and become such a person? Acting on my convictions ruined most every situation I found myself in. There had to be a different approach.

I walked beside my fellow vampires and the newly acquired youth, and maintained the passivity I'd chastised myself for moments ago.

***

The taller boy said, "I always wondered what this place looked like on the inside," once he stepped foot in our hotel room. "Nicer than the outside, I guess."

"Is it okay if I get high first?" said the shorter one. "I don't think I can look at it if I'm not high."

"Do whatever you want," said Daniel. He whispered something in Astrid's ear, and then addressed the boys again. "But blow it out the window, please."

"I'll be right back," said Astrid, and she disappeared outside.

I stuffed my hands in my pockets and tried to act casual. It didn't work. One of the boys offered me a hit from his bowl, and said, "Relax."

"How old are you?" I asked.

"Old enough," said the taller boy. "You want to smoke or what?"

"I quit," I said.

"How come?"

"I don't know. I guess it stopped making me feel good."

"That sucks," said the shorter boy.

Daniel opened the mini fridge. "Can I offer you anything while we wait? Astrid has to grab an organ from the car."

"What do you got?" said one of the boys.

"Bottled water, Coke, Diet Coke. That's about it, except for beer."

"I'll have a beer," said the shorter boy. "If that's cool with you."

Daniel hesitated, but tossed the boys a bottle. "You can share it."

The boys stayed by the window, and smoked and sipped their drink. Daniel and I sat on the bed. I started to drum blast beats with my fingers on the mattress. The motion released a bit of agitation.

"So what kind of movies do you make?" the taller boy asked me.

"Um, lots of kinds," I said, and rambled on. "Maybe not lots. They're all short films. The last one I directed was sort of experimental. It was inspired by this feminist film theorist, Laura Mulvey. You heard of her?"

The boys shook their heads.

"Oh," I said. "She claims that, like, women in cinema are sexual objects, and that the men who watch them have this sadistic gaze. In my film, I was trying to show a woman using her sexuality as a means of empowerment. But still from a male perspective."

The boys seemed bored by my explanation.

"Really, it was just a bondage movie shot in the forest," I said.

Daniel tried to move the conversation away from my stilted monologue. "You like movies?" he asked the boys.

"Sure," said the shorter one.

"What about vampire films?" said Daniel.

"I don't know," said the taller boy. "Name one."

Daniel turned the question towards me. "What's a good vampire film, David?"

"I couldn't tell you," I said, knowing full well that we used to watch them all the time.

"Really?" said Daniel, his tone incredulous. "My favorite was always *Nosferatu*. I'm a sucker for the classics."

"Never heard of it," said the shorter boy.

"It's before your time," I said.

"It's before our time too," said Daniel. "Doesn't mean we can't appreciate it."

"So when is that girl coming back?" said the taller boy. He appeared stoned, and paranoid because of it. "We probably have to go home soon."

"She'll be here soon," said Daniel. "It's worth the wait. I promise."

"Yeah, okay," said the taller boy.

"Can I talk to you?" I said to Daniel.

"I'm right here."

"No," I said. "In private."

The shorter boy took another hit from his pipe. "Are you guys going to, like, do something to us?"

"No," I said, and pulled Daniel from the bed. "Definitely not. But we're going outside for a minute, okay?" I pushed Daniel through the door and closed it behind us.

"What are you doing?"

His lack of eye contact furthered my suspicion: that he was

making things up as he went along.

"Well, where is Astrid?" I said.

"I told her to find an organ."

"You mean, you asked her to kill someone."

"Right," said Daniel.

"Fuck," I said. "Why would you do that?" I kept my words sharp and spiteful. Because I was building my defense. Just in case he tried to make me feel insignificant again. Or I might have been grappling with my petty machismo in order to appear, to him, as something other than weak. Daniel was the only person I wanted to be vulnerable with, and I couldn't even try. If only his post-human powers included a kind of telepathy. Then he would see my struggle, and love me despite it.

Why am I yelling at him?

Because what we're doing to these boys is wrong! Even if we haven't done it yet.

I clenched my fists, jaw, and an assortment of other muscles; readied myself for a fight that never came.

"Why are you here?" asked Daniel.

"Because Astrid drove me," I said, and tried to sound less upset.

Daniel stirred the gravel with his toe. "I know I asked her to bring you," he said. "But I'd hoped you wanted to come back. Or that being here would help you forgive me.

"I mean, all that stuff I told Astrid. About you and I raising an army together. I thought it would be cool to be something great with you. Again. But it's all kind of stupid, right?"

I hadn't planned to bring Daniel down. Not like that. I just wanted him to change his mind. To believe in a future other than Astrid's. From the sound of it, Daniel wanted the same thing that I did. He'd just taken the shittiest route to get back to me.

"Maybe it's not stupid," I said, and tried to reassure him. "But it's true there's no plan? You don't know how to convince those boys to be rule-abiding vampires any more than I do, right?"

"Everything else came so easily," said Daniel. "I thought I'd figure this part out when the time came." He threw his head towards the sky, in resignation. "But you're so fucking against doing this. So what's the point?"

"I don't know," I said, and felt like I needed to console him. "It's a lot of work for something you don't even believe in."

"Maybe," said Daniel. "But where do you think we came from? Astrid's explanation is the only one I've heard. At least, from an actual vampire. It sounds crazy, but so does anything else."

I hadn't meant to entertain an existential conversation. "Okay. If you really want to go there," I said. "If Astrid's right, then Christianity is right. Or partly right. That's a fucked up thing to believe, coming from us. Like, we'd really have to hate ourselves. There has to be a scientific explanation for what's happening to us. We have a virus, or something. I mean, have you even asked Astrid where she got that story?"

"Some old vampire," said Daniel. "She says he died a long time ago. Died for real."

"Didn't she say something about being able to tell truth from lies, and that's how she knew the story was real?"

Daniel nodded.

"But she believes you. And you haven't been all that truthful."

"I know," said Daniel.

"So maybe she was lied to," I said. "Or she made it all up."

"Made what up?" The voice came from several yards away. It was Astrid. She was breathing heavy and holding a blood-stained bag, stuffed with what appeared to be raw meat. "It's the best I could do on short notice," she said.

"What is it?" asked Daniel.

"A heart," said Astrid. Then her voice became weak. "What were you talking about?"

Neither of us would answer her.

"Where are the boys?" she said, and rushed to open the door.

"They're right where we left them," I said.

"I can see that," said Astrid.

"Is that..." The shorter boy tried to look inside the bag. "Well, what is it?"

Astrid looked to Daniel for guidance.

"Show them, I guess," said Daniel.

"It's a heart," said Astrid, as she extended the plastic bag.

The boys came to meet her in the doorway. "Why's it in a grocery bag?" said the taller boy.

"Can I touch it?" said the shorter boy. He didn't wait for an answer. "It's all warm."

"Uh, thanks for letting us see it," said the taller boy.

"Yeah, it was cool," said the shorter boy. "We should probably go, though. Our parents will be mad if we're not home soon."

They walked away from us, slowly at first. Then the taller boy fell into a sprint alongside his friend. We watched them disappear into the shadows of the towering, distant forest.

EVERY VAMP FOR HIMSELF

DANIEL BURIED HIS FACE IN HIS HANDS. ASTRID stared out the window at some far-off point in space. I hid in plain sight, and hoped that one of us would break the silence; hurry us towards an agreeable conclusion, an understanding that the whole excursion had been a big mistake.

Astrid spoke first. "Why did you ask me to do that? If it was going to be a waste?"

Daniel kept his head down, as if he hadn't heard her.

"I killed someone," said Astrid. "Not for food or some greater purpose. But to satisfy the curiosity of two little boys." She upped the ante and pointed her finger at me. "Did you convince Daniel to let the boys go? What else have you been doing behind my back?"

"What?"

"You are not a leader," said Astrid. "You're just standing in Daniel's way. And in the way of your salvation."

"He's not your leader either," I said, and raised my voice.

"You weren't around to witness all he's done," said Astrid. "You think you know everything about him, but you have no idea."

"Stop it," said Daniel. He sat up and pleaded softly. "Please."

We stopped shouting, and waited for his guidance, like

Daniel was the one who still knew what to do.

"I'm sorry," said Astrid.

"There's no plan," said Daniel. "There never was."

Astrid looked like she'd bitten into rotten food. "Maybe it's too soon. You've done so much already, and things can't always go at the pace we'd like. You have to wait for it to come to you. I know it will."

"You don't understand," said Daniel. He looked to me, as if I might help explain.

I considered that he might have wanted to turn the world's population into vampires set on doing his bidding. If he'd come up with a strategy, he might have even followed through. But I was the closest thing to a trial run. It had been enough trouble keeping me in line.

"I'm no leader," said Daniel. "I doubt that David is either."

"Don't say that. It's just this friend..." Astrid twisted the word so that its meaning was all but erased. "...Of yours putting thoughts into your head. I know he whispers about me when I'm not close enough to hear. I know he makes you doubt me, makes you doubt yourself."

"I made everything up," said Daniel. "Everything that's happened so far has been a fucking fluke."

"You're upset," said Astrid, pleading. "That's all. Things didn't work out today, but did you expect them to? Give it time. The path will lay itself out."

I tried to intervene, polite as I could manage. "Would you just listen to him?"

She scowled at me and bore her teeth, like an animal. Then she returned to Daniel, and caressed him with words and touch.

But Daniel had given up. "There's not going to be any army. Not because of me."

"Remember who stood by you these past years," said Astrid, nearly in tears. "Don't give up on me now." She held Daniel's hands and hair, and tried to force his head up so that he'd look at her.

Eventually, Astrid climbed on to the bed and wept alone. She said something into the pillow, like, "I'll wait another hundred years if I have to."

I crawled past her, and found my way to Daniel. But when I reached out to touch him, he fought my hands away.

It seemed redundant to join in their grieving, so I left Daniel and Astrid, and went for a walk to clear my head. I wandered towards the forest and picked the first trail I saw. The path turned into un-forged terrain – dirt, leaves, and underbrush. I kept on going until I no longer cared where I'd end up.

A WALK IN THE PARK

THE WOODS DIDN'T LAST AS LONG AS THEY USED to. I found the end of the tree line at the beginning of a large construction site. I wasn't sure what purpose the structure would serve, but the boxes inside suggested an array of offices or small retail stores.

I walked through the unfinished parking lot and peered down the converging road. There was a gas station in sight. One that I recognized. It seemed like a good enough place to find a snack. I hadn't eaten since breakfast, and my blood-lust was returning. A piece of jerky or other processed animal flesh seemed like it might remind me of the juice it once soaked in. Or would animal blood even satisfy my hunger? Was human plasma the only drink that would fill me up?

I bought a piece of jerky and took a bite. The meat felt like paper in my stomach.

I lingered near the payphone, outside the gas station, and considered making an inappropriate call. Mika would surely hang up if she heard my voice on the other line. But would she stay long enough to listen to another one of my apologies? I could assure her that I'd been successful. That no more harm would befall her, or anyone around her. At least, not by the hands or mouths of fanged creatures.

My optimism took hold of me. I dialed Mika's number before I could come up with anything to say. By the time I heard the first ring, I felt foolish and worse.

"Hello?" said Mika, croaked from the other line.

"Mika, it's David. Please don't hang up." I heard something near to silence, but not a dead line. Her breath was still present, crackling through the receiver. "You there?" I asked, and hoped that she hadn't abandoned me so quickly.

There was a sound, like a swallow and the smack of lips, wet with saliva.

"I'm so sorry," I said. "For everything. But it's all over now."

"Where are you?" said Mika.

"I've gone home."

"To your parents?"

"No."

"Where are you staying?" said Mika. She was so insistent on the question that I began to wonder why. Was she even the one asking?

"Some hotel around here," I said.

"You mean in Grass Valley?" said Mika, her voice flat.

"Well..." I started to tell her that I was staying in the nearby town, Nevada City. But something in her voice was off. I no longer trusted her.

"Just a minute," said Mika. The phone crackled more than usual. Her breath disappeared, or sounded distant. I could hear the whispers of another voice. At first, I thought it was interference from a separate phone line. The longer I listened, the more it sounded like the voice was coming from beside Mika. She was with someone else. And that person was giving her advice on what to say. If Mika was following along, that person definitely wanted to know where I was.

"David? Are you still there?" Mika returned with more confidence. "David, I need to know the name of the hotel. The one you're staying at."

I hung up and berated myself. Of course, with all that had happened, Mika had gone to the police. They were the ones prodding her for information about where, exactly, I might have been.

I raced back into the woods, and towards the hotel. If I'd given up my location, I had to warn Daniel. And, I guess, Astrid too.

WHEN THE ALARM SOUNDS

ASTRID WAS ON THE BED, SNORING. DANIEL HAD fallen back in his chair. Drool dripped from his lip and on to the faux-leather surface.

I turned on the lights and rushed to Daniel's side. I was able to wake him up with a few, heavy shakes.

"They're coming," I said. "We have to get out of here."

"Who?" said Daniel, yawning.

"The police." I tossed the sheets that covered Astrid, and rocked her back and forth. "Get up. We have to go. Now!"

"Stop it," said Astrid. She wouldn't open her eyes.

"What did you do?" asked Daniel, still slumped in his chair.

"Are you kidding?" I said, as if the whole world had known my crimes. "I killed someone. You killed someone. We're all guilty of murder."

"I'm going to kill you if you don't shut up," said Astrid. She pushed her head between two pillows, using them as giant earplugs.

"How do the police know you're here?" asked Daniel.

"It doesn't matter," I said.

"It does."

"Fine," I said, to hurry him. "I called my friend, Mika. And I'm pretty sure she had cops with her."

"You told them where you are?" said Daniel.

"Not exactly," I said. "But she knows I'm in the area."

Astrid bolted up in bed. "Do I have to spell it out for you?" she said. "We are not wanted by the police." She motioned between Daniel and herself. "You are the only one. I don't care what happens to you. Not anymore."

Daniel was less harsh. "Relax," he said. "What's the worst that they can do?"

"Aren't you guys worried that they might suspect you, or something?" I said.

"No," said Astrid. "Not unless you plan on giving up our names."

"Astrid," I said, in hopes to calm her. "I wouldn't..."

"I know," she said. "Or else I really would kill you."

Daniel leaned back into his chair. "We'll talk about it in the morning," he said. "This has been too fucked up of a day."

I was in awe at the response to my intended good will. I'd only meant to protect my friend. But I'd become unworthy of both excitement and alarm.

What will you do?

Run.

Where?

Away from California. Maybe away from the country. I have the whole rest of the world to explore.

But where can you settle down? The need to eat will come, and you'll have to run again.

What are my other options?

Stop running.

But that means...

***

I spent the rest of the night sipping blood from medical packets. The blue and red lights didn't come flashing until dawn.

I washed my face in the bathroom, and pushed my wet fingers through my hair. My eyes stayed dry as I looked at Daniel for – what I thought would be – the last time.

Then I wandered outside, my hands to the sky as I walked towards the black and white cars. There were pistols drawn from behind the vehicular barriers. The uniformed men rushed towards me, and I fell to my knees in defeat.

I accepted every form of captivity forced upon me.

LOVE, DAVID

DEAR DANIEL,

I hope this letter finds you well, if it finds you at all. I'm not sure if it's addressed correctly. All I have to go off of is memory, and I'm not even sure if you live in the same apartment.

If this letter ends up in the hands of Daniel Brion, I want to say, "I'm sorry." I wish things could have turned out another way.

I've spent the past three months at the Folsom State Penitentiary. There was a short trial before, in which I confessed to all the violence I'd done. But with no mention of vampires.

I want you to know that I never implicated you. Or Astrid. Or Ian. I've decided the punishment is mine alone. Even though I spend some nights putting blame on everyone else.

When I first arrived here, the guards assessed me as something of a hazard. "Fresh meat," so to speak. They put me in a cell with a young man named Charles. So young, he looked like a boy.

Charles was always crying. Sometimes, after a trip to the shower, he'd disappear. Often for days at a time. He'd come back with cuts and bruises, and say that he'd been at the infirmary. It was easy enough to assume that he was regularly raped and beaten.

I chose Charles as my first "real" prison meal. I hadn't tasted blood for weeks, and felt like I was starving. Charles seemed so dis-

couraged by his own life. He often talked of suicide. I thought that I was doing him a favor.

One night, I climbed down from my bunk and bit into his neck. I don't know why, but I didn't cover his mouth or sever his vocal cords. He screamed while I drank his blood.

The guards arrived and beat me off of him. Charles was sent the infirmary again. I was put in solitary confinement.

I spent the next week trying to come up with ways to feed myself. Nothing seemed practical. Nothing that would last more than a few days.

Then I was released back into the general population.

I heard whispers about Charles. That he'd become a kind of monster. It seemed that he'd survived my bite and completed his transformation. I heard that he'd been attacked, but that he'd fought back and won. The inmate who'd put hands on him had been killed and bled dry.

So Charles was put in solitary around the time I was getting out. But not before he'd spread the word that I was responsible for his new strength and blood-lust.

My first day back in the prison yard was one of the strangest of my life. I mean that after all that's happened. Some of the largest men I'd ever seen knelt down at my feet and begged. They wanted me to bite them. I must have drank from fifty men that day. As hungry as I was, I didn't stop to think of the consequences.

I'm not sure how many have died. But the disease, or curse, or whatever it is; it's spreading faster than it's taking people's lives. It seems like half the prison population's become like us. The rest will be changed or eaten soon. At some point, our source of food will disappear. We'll have no choice but to escape. The guards won't stand a chance.

Why haven't we broken out already? What's keeping the prison-

ers here if they've no doubt discovered their strength and near-immortality? The answer seems to be that they're waiting for me.

I didn't realize it at first. But the gang-like hierarchy that prevails here has put me in a unique position. Before I arrived, no one was capable of the things they are now. No one had that sort of power. I've become heralded as a kind of godfather, patient zero for the prison's vampire strain. Members from rival gangs have come together under a new blanket of influence. They're no longer constrained by region or ethnic background. Their blood bonds them together now. And they look to me as the source of their new life and for the meaning behind it.

I haven't done anything to sway them. In fact, I may have encouraged their praise. I understand, now, how easy it was for you to become Astrid's savior. It feels good to be treated like a king.

But I'm scared.

The situation here is beginning to sound a lot like Astrid's "prophecy." I'm raising something like an army. These people actually listen to me. It remains to be seen whether I'll have the same effect outside the prison.

Anyway, it looks like I'll be getting out of here soon. Let me know where I can find you?

Maybe you could spare some thoughts on my situation, which will likely include you in the near future. People keep asking me what we are. I feel some kind of pressure to deliver Astrid's explanation. If for no other reason than it's the only story I have to tell.

I guess that's it for now. The only thing left to say is that I miss you.

Love,
David

YOUR FRIEND

DAVID,

I got your letter. I'm still in San Francisco. So are Astrid and Ian. I hadn't spoken to either of them for a while. Astrid said she hated me after what happened up north. She called me a fraud and said worse things about you. I guess I wasn't happy with you either, what with you taking off like that. But I didn't realize you were in jail.

I took a few days to think about it before I shared your letter. To be honest, it didn't have much to do with you. I don't have anyone to talk to these days. I thought that if Astrid could get excited about her vampire crusades again, she might forgive me or something.

So I gave her your letter. She still thinks I'm a fraud. But she seems convinced that you're the one she's been talking about all this time. Take it for what you will. If you want to start acting like a vampire messiah, my advice is to not let anyone down. You have more people looking up to you than I did. They sound more likely to fuck you up if you turn out to be a fake.

Do what you want. I'm not convinced of anything anymore. It could be a fluke, or you could be the destruction of Heaven and all that. I guess I'll have to wait until the day someone stakes me through the heart. Or you kill God.

Astrid will probably try to visit you soon. Let's just say that, unless things change, I'll see you when you get out. Come find me at my apartment. I'll be here. For better or worse.

Your friend,
Daniel

EXODUS

DANIEL'S LETTER ARRIVED THE SAME DAY THAT the inmates planned to escape. My blood ran hot with excitement until I finished reading.

Where I had written, "Love," Daniel had addressed me as a mere friend. It occurred to me that his emotions had become so susceptible to circumstance that I'd never be able to rely on more than a fleeting gesture of his affection. He left me years ago on the chance that vampires might exist, and he was leaving me again, even if he didn't know it. Was it depression? The idea that I'd replaced him as a martyr? Or had he simply lost interest – grown tired of me despite the steel, concrete, and hundreds of miles between us?

Sure, I'd left him too. But it was a matter of necessity; tumultuous circumstance.

I thought that my letter had suggested hope for us. After reading Daniel's note, it was clear that he'd given up.

He was only one man. My fellow inmates – with their separate goals and agendas – would surely leave me sooner. I wasn't exactly invested in them. But the thought of recycled abandonment weighed heavy on my chest.

I felt no joy or motivation as the men tore us from our prison. The inmates slaughtered guards. They took bullets to their bodies, and laughed as they kept forward. I heard the music of machinery destroyed, cells ripped apart, and men chanting for freedom. It seemed like a kind of revolution I'd once watched on television. And it was mine. Still, I spent the day slumped over my bed with Daniel's letter in my lap.

The chaos simmered to a rumble of casual violence.

My first cellmate, Charles, stood by the door like a showman ushering me in for the final act. Except he didn't look the part. His face and clothing were spattered with red flecks and accentuated by the lines of drying blood. Amidst the evidence of carnage, he smiled at me, as if to say, "We did it."

I couldn't smile back. I felt like a decrepit despot, who had to crawl, or else be wheeled, towards the vision of his own empire.

"What's wrong?" said Charles.

I didn't answer.

He lead me down a path littered with remnants of destruction: bodies without wrappers, smashed security cameras sprinkled about like sharp candy, papers, trinkets, and other trash that inmates used to pride as their belongings.

Beyond the outer walls, we were thrust into the mob. A congregation of men rioted in celebration of the instincts that had rescued them from bondage.

A circle grew at the edge of the crowd. Cries of awe referenced someone new. For many of the men, it had been years since they'd laid eyes on a woman. But there she was, brushing off the advances of all who dared come near her.

She seemed to have gained some of their respect, because she'd matched the strength of more than a dozen men. I recognized her voice as she shouted above the drone of male tongues. It was Astrid, a reformed believer in my ability to change the course of history.

I pushed my way towards her, and did my best to camouflage myself within the horde.

Astrid threw several men beneath her and climbed on to their backs. When she was at least a head above the rest, she shouted, "Quiet, all of you! This is no time for celebration. Your battles have just begun. You think because you've escaped this prison, you're free? You think no one's noticed? The police, the military, the national guard; they're all on their way."

"We can fucking take them," heckled one man.

"Maybe," said Astrid. "But what of your greatest foe?"

"Who the fuck are you?" shouted another.

"Get down, you fucking cunt!"

The voices could have been comprised of one or twenty men. It didn't matter. What was spoken aloud spread like wildfire. The mob became a single fury that Astrid did her best to take hold of.

She screamed at them louder than before. "Who do you think you are? All of you. Not as individuals, but as vampires. What do you think that means?"

"We know what we are," shouted a convict. "And we could tear you apart."

"Come and try it," said Astrid. She fell into attack position, but no man budged from his place. "I'm a vampire too. Only, I've lived long enough to know how to survive, adapt when necessary, and surely take on the likes of you." She pointed her finger, as if she knew each man who would cross her. "The fact is that you need me. All of you. If it makes you feel better, I also need you."

"We have the man we need!"

"David Nevenhart?" said Astrid. "Is that who you have?" The air changed. A sea of gasps rang off the concrete walls.

"Who are you?"

"My name is Astrid. I'm an old friend of David's. You're right to think of him as your leader. He's the reason you're not still locked in your cages. But David is more than just your prison chief. He will lead you beyond this life and into your rightful place in eternity." Astrid let her sermon sink into the minds of several thousand men. Unlike the preachers who spoke to them on Sundays, Astrid had the luxury of tangible proof. Each man had witnessed the transformation of his body.

"Where is your David Nevenhart?" said Astrid.

The men nearest to me raised my arms, as if presenting a fighter. They looked at me with an unwavering belief that I would know what to do; watched my reaction to gauge what theirs should be.

They pushed me forward until I stood in Astrid's shadow. The soap-box preaching vampire came down from her podium of men.

Astrid wrapped her arms around me and held me like her life depended on it. I hadn't even acted, and she'd won the convicts over – established a bond between their history and hers.

Words of gratitude dropped into my ear. Astrid apologized for having ever doubted me. She said that I should rest, and that she would take on the burden of explanation. And she did. She told the men the same story that she'd told me: of Heaven and Hell, Jesus and Lucifer, and the battle we should wage on God.

Astrid pruned the convicts to do her bidding, and reinforced their belief in me. I tried, but couldn't bring myself to feel anger at what she said. Even if the men left me, I was grateful for their temporary devotion.

The speech ended, and the men remained quiet and still. They seemed eager to receive their next instruction.

Astrid took me by the arm. We walked away from the prison. The men followed.

I closed my eyes, and imagined Daniel as the one beside me. But the terrain was treacherous, and I had to look out for sticks and rocks beneath my feet. To move forward, I could only spend a second at a time lost in my dreams. Only a second at a time with the boy who occupied them.

CONVINCING STORY

I STARED OUT THE DOOR OF A QUAINT, SUBURBAN home. It was near dusk, and I could see through the windows of the houses across the street. Each one contained a dead or transformed family. Each one harbored a group of convicts who'd taken quarter for the night.

I wasn't sure if Astrid had chosen the neighborhood, specifically. Her coup could have been exercised in any residential village.

The homeowners didn't have time to call for help. There was no interruption, no interference, and nothing to stand in our way. It was a quiet invasion, over in minutes.

Only in the aftermath did I witness the terror brought upon the families. A woman, in the house across from where I stood, was tossed around a kitchen, toyed with and splayed for the men I used to consort with in mess halls and prison yards. Down the street, a man's arms were ripped from his body and made into a feast. If the violence was evidence of things to come, I couldn't imagine why anyone would join us.

"David?" It was Astrid's voice, somewhere behind me.

I turned. "How long have you been standing there?'

"Just a moment," she said. "And you?"

I glanced back to the rows of windows, and to what took

place beyond them. "I don't know."

"Does it bother you?" she said. "What they're doing?"

"It doesn't bother you?"

"It's a war, David. We've been given violent men to wage it."

I stepped back from the door and closed it. "What makes you think this is a war?" I said. "I mean, you weren't alive two thousand years ago. You didn't see Jesus in the desert. Who told you these things were true?"

"David, you've come closer to fulfilling our purpose than anyone I've met, and you still question everything around you."

"I see what's around me. We're vampires. I get it. But there's nothing to suggest the hand of God or Lucifer, or anything like that."

Astrid leaned herself against the wall, as if to gain support for her convictions. "I'll tell you what you want to hear. But consider what you've seen and what you've been through. Ask yourself, 'What keeps you from believing?'"

I pondered her suggestion. Why had I been so opposed to her story? After all, there'd been no proposed alternative. I lacked the scientific knowledge to understand whether my body could have changed by means of a biological reaction. Was a supernatural cause so wrong to consider? It seemed strange to think my flesh was somehow bound to a Christian doctrine. I maintained my skepticism, but allowed room for what Astrid had to say.

"Remember, during our car ride from San Francisco," said Astrid. "I told you of my first love. Of Gottfried and our journey to America?"

I nodded.

"Do you remember where I left off?"

I said, with some certainty, "You told me that you ate a passenger on a ship. That you were caught."

“I’d have to finish the story to answer your question,” said Astrid. “If that’s alright with you.”

“Of course.”

“We were sailing from Germany to a port in Massachusetts,” said Astrid. “Some of the ship’s crew were natives of that state. They told the captain tales of witches who lived in the town of Salem a hundred, or so, years prior.”

“You mean the Salem witch trials?” I said. “You know those were all bogus, right?”

“Maybe,” said Astrid. “But the men had nothing else to think of me. The passengers were frightened. Many wanted to throw me overboard. Gottfried did his best to stop them. He convinced the captain to lock me in a cage meant for traveling livestock. I stayed there for days on end while the crew tried to figure out what sort of devil I could be.”

“What did you tell them?”

“What could I tell them? I protested, sure, and asked for Gottfried when conditions became unbearable. He rarely came. Even when he stopped the crew from drowning me, he never looked me in the eye.

“Once in Massachusetts, they took me to a constable. They said I was a witch. That I was in league with the devil.

“Burnings were no longer common place. But they made an exception for me. There was no trial. I was locked away until it was my time to burn at the stake.

“At that point in my life, I was sure that I was different. I hadn’t aged in decades. But I’d never considered immortality. If fire meant death for witches, I thought it might mean the same for me.

“When the flames took my skin...” I saw a pain in Astrid, and almost felt a heat come off of her. “When they reached my eyes, I had a vision. You've heard people talk of near-death experiences? A dark tunnel followed by a white light? I saw nothing like that. At the edge of death, I peered into Hell." Her eyes glazed over, and she was lost in her memory. "I don't ever want to go back there."

I had so many questions – about what she saw and how she knew that it existed outside her imagination. But I was struck by some desire to comfort her. Whether or not she glimpsed Hell, I could only imagine that her torture was extraordinary. Even for a vampire. I reached out and nearly touched her. She continued on before my fingers grazed her skin.

"I couldn't see in front of me," said Astrid. "Not anything from this world. My eyes had burned out. So had the ropes that bound me. I ran from the fire and from the demons in that other place." She let out something like a laugh, but one removed from joy. "It's almost funny, now, to think of it. A skinless woman running through the streets.

"What happened next was a miracle by any standard. A man tackled me in the woods outside the town. A man who was also a vampire. Can you believe it? He'd come to America years before. When he saw me, he knew instantly that we were the same.

"I thought he was trying to kill me at first, so I fought back. He had to tie me up and wait until I was asleep from exhaustion. When I woke, he was spoon-feeding me blood from his bedside table. He nursed me back to health.

"I don't mean to bog you down with more names from my past. But this man was very important to me. His name was Cyrus, and I suppose he was my second love. Our relationship was platonic. Cyrus had no interest in my body. He only sought me as a companion; someone who could share his secret. He'd been bitten much later in his life, and so appeared old, like he could have been my father. In many ways, he was.

"When Cyrus told me of our origin, I believed him. It wasn't his nature to lie. He lived a simple life. He wasn't trying to do what we are now. There was no ulterior motive I could tell. He meant to educate me, but also to protect me from those who might kill us.

"Back then, there were still men who sought to hunt monsters and demons. I know it because they staked poor Cyrus through the heart. It was on the eve of the journey we would have taken together. Out here. Out west."

Astrid struggled against tears. "There's no more proof in my story than in what I told you before. But there's something to be said for acknowledging your own experience in light of what you've seen and heard. There's a reason I saw into Hell. It's because part of that place lives in me. It lives in you too."

"I'm sorry for all you've gone through," I said. "And maybe you're right, but..."

"But what?"

"I'm not into hurting people," I said. "Not on purpose."

Astrid shook her head. "To eat, you will kill. And if you don't kill, you will uproot people's lives. There is always hurt."

"You're the one who led those men here," I said. "Why do I have to be their leader?"

"You're saying that I should do it myself?"

"If you want to," I said. "But I don't think that I can help. I'm not Cyrus, or Gottfried, or any of those people you loved. The person I want by my side is Daniel."

"I know," said Astrid. I could see that she wanted to say more.

"I'm sorry."

Astrid walked into the center of the house and was consumed

by the darkness of its innermost rooms. I turned the other way and set my sights for San Francisco.

DREAMS OF FORGOTTEN MEN

I'D TRAVELED A LONG WAY TO SEE DANIEL, AND thought of many things to tell him. But standing outside his door, the distance still seemed vast. All I'd meant to say to him had disappeared from my head.

I knocked, and waited for an invitation into his apartment, his home, his heart. There was no response. But I'd given up so much to be at Daniel's door, and couldn't let it be the end. Not without pushing further.

My weight crashed against the door. Wood splintered around the lock. I went inside, beyond the foyer, and found that the light bulbs had been broken or burned out. Then I brought a hand to my nose, in instinct – to shield myself from the stench of death.

I could barely see, and so crawled on my hands and knees, and felt the marble floor turn to a crusted surface that took on moisture with closer proximity to the bedroom. Near the edge of a wall, I dropped my hands into the swampy marsh of skin and decomposing organs. I no longer feared such things. But I took a breath and ran my palms along the carcass. I needed to know that the body belonged to someone other than my friend.

A woman's breasts sat above the ribs. So I ventured on with some relief, and discovered more corpses along the way.

White light sparkled off a bit of moisture, hung to glass. It was Daniel's bedroom window. I stood up and stumbled forward, and found Daniel, awash in moonlight, splayed at the foot of his bed.

I rushed to his side, frightened that I'd find him frozen and lifeless. But blood pumped warm through his veins. His chest moved with the rhythm of his shallow breath.

"Daniel," I said, whispered, as if a greater noise might break him. I nudged him, but he wouldn't move. On my final push, I saw a brief reflection in his open eyes. "I came as soon as I could."

His stare was cold and blank, and aimed somewhere along the floor. What I'd felt when I'd read his letter was amplified by his passivity.

Still, I hung on to the possibility that I'd offended him by something other than my presence. "I knocked. There was no answer."

"I know," said Daniel, the first of his acknowledgements.

The piled corpses, the lack of light or any electrical circuit in the apartment, Daniel's fetal position on the floor; it all served as evidence of his collapse. As a child, I'd rarely seen him somber, let alone in the grips of depression. But there he was, like an empty shell, or a man upon his deathbed.

"Do you want me to leave?" I asked.

Daniel didn't say a word, but I thought I saw him shrug. So I returned, for a while, to the darkness of his living room.

I couldn't do it in front of him. Didn't even want to let him hear. I cried silently among his victims, barely a hundred feet from the ghost of the boy I loved. My face turned wet, and I felt like I was drowning. The sensation forced me to fight, to keep from going under.

I dragged myself back towards Daniel's room, and sat as close to him as I could. "You have no right to do this," I said.

"What?" said Daniel, as if he hadn't heard me.

"You turned me into a monster," I said. "I still came back for you."

"You'll get over it."

"What the fuck is wrong with you?"

"I don't have a life," said Daniel. "And I have to live it forever."

That was his excuse? He could treat me any way he wanted because our time on earth might not end? Any act could be forgiven, or at least forgotten, with the passing years?

My brain screamed for me to loathe every inch of the boy before me. But I remained ill at the thought of losing him. I was addicted to his scent, his sound, and the promise of his skin.

"Not so long ago," I said, "you offered me the world. With you and I together, doing anything we wanted."

"Give it up," said Daniel. "You were right. I don't know you anymore, and you don't know me. Neither of us got what we wanted." His words were muffled and sterile, barely whispered into the ground.

"Then give me my fucking life back!" I punched my fist into his chest, and saw that he didn't move. So I stood and turned my back to him, and found my way through the maze of his living room. I cried down the stairwell, and ran into the streets; kept running until I tired, and then fell into a gutter.

Around me, I saw vagrants, asleep under piles of trash. Some looked cold and others peaceful. I wondered if they dreamed about what could have been, and also of their death.

I pulled my jacket tight around me, and joined the homeless in their slumber.

THE BEGINNING AND THE END

THE MORNING CAME WITH SIRENS AND A LOW rumble that rocked my head against the ground. A man in tattered jeans and a filthy overcoat shook me from my sleep. "Up, up," he said. "They're clearing the streets. All of them."

"Who?" I asked.

The man pointed down the street. "They say we're readying for an attack. I would've thought terrorists, but now I can't figure out what kind. They say they're coming from the north."

I looked to where the man had pointed, and saw an approaching military tank and a convoy of U.S. soldiers.

"When the army takes over, you get no trial," said the man. "Come on. The shelters are taking everyone in."

I waved him away, and said, "I'll be a minute."

"It's your skin," he said, and shuffled away.

The rest of the vagrants had already left. I was the only one who remained in plain view. One of the foot soldiers spotted me and raised a megaphone to his mouth. "Evacuate the streets, civilian! This is your first and final warning!"

"Why?" I shouted. "What's happened?" I had to know if the military had come for the reasons I assumed. Had news of our escape traveled so quickly? Had Astrid moved on to more of her conquest?

"It's for your own safety," said the soldier. "Evacuate immediately."

"I have a right to know," I said, and stood my ground.

Two soldiers broke from the pack and came jogging towards me. "Man, what are you doing?" said one, when he was near. "Get the fuck off the street or you're going to end up in the hole for a real long time. Understand?"

I understood fine. But there was nothing left that he could do to hurt me. "It's important," I said. "I need to know what's going on."

"You need to shut the fuck up and start moving," said the other soldier.

I spat at his feet and stood still. I'd been torn, against my will, from the rank of civilians. If the soldiers planned to take their orders any further, they'd find out what I'd become.

The soldiers raised their guns and pointed them at me. I jumped towards the men and ripped into their necks. I took chunks from their arteries, esophagi, and the surrounding tendons. There were barely any screams before the men fell, clutching their throats.

"He's one of them!"

"It's a bleeder!"

I heard shouts amidst the onslaught of muzzle bursts and whizzing bullets. Bits of searing metal tore into my stomach, chest, and face. Pieces of my body split open, tore off, and exploded into mists of organic matter.

My skull cracked open and my brain was turned to soup. It was strange to know that I existed despite how much of me had been removed.

I no longer knew what I was or what space I occupied. I couldn't see, smell, taste, touch, or hear a thing. There was a void all around me. Or I'd become the void.

But there was a sensation. Something like fear. I dreaded my unknown future, and felt lost without my flesh. And though I didn't want to believe it, I considered where I traveled – to a place that I'd called Hell.

I'm frightened.

Frightened of what?

I don't know, but it feels like the worst fear of all. I only know what I left behind: a legacy of violence and despair. No one likely cares whether I existed then or now. If someone feels a way about me, it's because I caused them harm.

A presence surrounded me. It wasn't light, because I had no way to see it. And it wasn't warm, because I had no nerves to feel. Though, if I could describe it, I'd say it was light and warm and pulling me towards it.

Slowly, there were senses that I recognized from life. A haze, like my old vision, and the pain of skin on fire.

A clarity did come, and I saw a world of so much horror. All at once, I believed in Astrid – at least a part of what she'd said. I prayed, from the abyss, that I'd come back to life. Then I prayed a while longer that Astrid's victory was near.

CHRISTOPHER ZEISCHEGG is a writer, musician, and filmmaker who spent eight years working in the adult film industry as performer, Danny Wylde.

He's the author of three books, *Come to my Brother*, *The Wolves that Live in Skin and Space*, and *Body to Job*, and has contributed to the *The Feminist Porn Book*, *Best Sex Writing*, *Coming Out Like a Porn Star*, *Split Lips*, and a variety of digital publications, such as *Somesuch* and *Nerve*.

Zeischegg lives in Los Angeles with his two cats, Victoria and Isis.